Pixie Was Going to Jump the Fence!

Megan sat up one more time and gave a last desperate yank on the reins. But her arms felt weak, and her legs were beginning to tremble. Pixie didn't slow down at all. The paddock fence loomed before her.

Pixie sailed over the fence, crossed the paddock in several strides, and jumped out. Megan managed to stay on, although she had never jumped a fence that high in her life. . . . Megan realized that if she didn't stop, Pixie would surely gallop right down the barn aisle and maybe hurt someone. She tried again to stop her, but it was no use.

"Pulley rein! Use the pulley rein!" she heard someone shout. . . .

Suddenly Megan remembered. She grabbed the mane with one hand and sat back. With the other hand she yanked the rein up and back as hard as she could several times in a row. To her relief she felt Pixie slow down. . . .

All during the terrifying bolt, the only thing Megan could hear was the sound of Pixie's feet drumming the earth. Now that she had stopped, everything seemed so quiet. Then Megan realized she could hear her own heart pounding louder and louder. She had hung on all that time, but now she felt herself slipping out of the saddle. . . .

Books in the SHORT STIRRUP CLUB™ series (by Allison Estes)

#1 Blue Ribbon Friends
#2 Ghost of Thistle Ridge

Available from MINSTREL BOOKS

Blue Ribbon Friends

Allison Estes

A
MINSTREL®
BOOK

Published by POCKET BOOKS
New York London Toronto Sydney Tokyo Singapore

A MINSTREL PAPERBACK *Original*

 A Minstrel Book published by
POCKET BOOKS, a division of Simon & Schuster Inc.
1230 Avenue of the Americas, New York, NY 10020

Copyright © 1996 by Allison Estes

ISBN: 0-671-54516-7

First Minstrel Books printing June 1996

10 9 8 7 6 5 4 3 2 1

SHORT STIRRUP CLUB is a trademark of Simon & Schuster Inc.

A MINSTREL BOOK and colophon are registered trademarks of
Simon & Schuster Inc.

Cover photo by Pat Hill; shot on location
at Overpeck Riding Academy, New Jersey

Printed in the U.S.A.

To my grandfather, Albert Jetton, who put me on a horse when I was four years old.

"Short Stirrup" is a division in horse shows, open to riders age twelve and under. Additional requirements may vary from show to show.

1

"THERE IT IS!" MEGAN MORRISON, AGE ELEVEN, pressed her face close to the tinted window in the back seat of her parents' dark green Bronco. Her brown eyes sparkled with excitement. A lock of curly brown hair had escaped from her ponytail, and she tucked it impatiently behind her ear.

"Look, Max," she commanded.

Megan's twin brother, Max, leaned across his sister's lap as far as the seat belt would allow him and scanned the landscape. They were driving down a paved road lined on both sides by a white wooden fence. Beyond the fence, nearly as far as they could see were hilly green pastures, broken here and there by shimmering ponds. Stands of pine and huge, old pin oak trees spread islands of shade where horses could escape from the summer sun.

1

"I see it," Max said, not sounding particularly excited.

"Dad, slow down!" Megan squealed. "You're going to miss the turn!"

James Morrison, the twins' father, glanced over his shoulder at his daughter. Megan had inherited his handsome, round face and thick, wavy hair. In fact, she looked more like her father than her twin. Max had his mother's light hair and her tall, slim build.

"Meg, Meg, calm down," James Morrison said with a laugh. "I'm not going to miss it—see? We're slowing down . . . we're turning into the driveway . . . and here we are." He stopped the Bronco.

Megan and Max looked up at a green sign hanging by two chains from a cedar post. In the center of the sign, outlined in gold, was a horse jumping over a spiky plant. The black and gold letters above read "Thistle Ridge Farm."

"This is it, Max!" Megan grabbed her brother's arm excitedly. "This is our new barn! Oh, I can't wait to see Pixie! I miss her so much! I hope she and Popsicle made the trip okay."

Pixie, Megan's gray pony mare, and Popsicle, Max's chestnut quarter-horse gelding, had left in the horse trailer two days before. They should have arrived at the new barn by now.

"Megan, you're cutting off the circulation in my arm," Max said patiently.

"Sorry!" She let go of his arm and undid her seat belt. "You didn't tell us this place was so big," she said, hanging over the front seat between her parents. "It looks like something from a movie!"

Dr. Rose Morrison closed the thick book she had been reading. She pulled her sunglasses down and peered over them at her son and daughter. "I told you it was nice." She smiled. "What do you think, Max?"

"It's okay," he mumbled.

"Okay?" Megan looked at her brother in amazement. She knew Max hadn't been happy about moving, but she couldn't believe he wasn't even a *little* bit interested in the new barn. "It's *awesome*, Mom," Megan said, gazing at the acres and acres of pasture sprawling all around them. The farm in Connecticut where they'd always kept her pony and her brother's horse was nowhere near this big.

They went on, up a long gravel drive lined with stately pecan trees. On either side were white-fenced paddocks. In some of them, groups of horses grazed peacefully.

"I wonder where the ring is," said Megan. "I can't wait to see the jumps! Mom, do they have horse shows at this barn?"

Max actually perked up at the thought of showing. "Do they, Mom? What did the manager say when you spoke to him?" he asked.

"He didn't say. But if they don't run shows at this barn, there are bound to be local shows you can go to. We'll find out, okay?"

"Mom, Look! Look, Max!" Megan said.

"What is it?" her mother asked, looking around.

"Look where?" Max wanted to know.

"There! In the paddock!" Megan was pointing to the last paddock on the left, closest to the main barn. "Ooooh, aren't they cuuute?"

In the paddock were four little foals, all turned out to play together. Two were reddish-colored chestnuts with white socks. Another was white with big brown spots. These three were dashing around on their long, spindly legs and hopping into the air practicing tiny bucks. They must have been used to seeing cars because they didn't stop their game for a second as the Bronco pulled up beside the paddock.

"Oh, look at the little paint!" Max pointed to the white-and-brown colt, who kicked up his heels so far he almost lost his balance. He ended up turning completely around in the air, very nearly landing on his nose. For the first time in quite a while, Max smiled. "Which one do you like, Meg?" he asked her.

"The bay! Oh, isn't she beautiful?" The fourth baby was very dark brown, with a perfect crescent moon on her forehead. She had stopped playing with the others and stood watching the Bronco, her big brown eyes curious and unafraid. She seemed to be looking right at Megan.

"Max, roll down your window," Megan begged. She leaned over Max and stuck her head out the window. "Here, baby . . . here, pretty," she called in a soft voice. She made a clucking sound.

The filly took a step forward, as if she might be

4

interested in making friends. Then, in a second, she spun on her little haunches and galloped away down the fence line as hard as she could go.

"She is *so cute,*" Megan said, watching the little filly join her playmates at the end of the paddock.

"I still like the paint," said Max.

"That's good, Max, because when we get to the new house, you are going to be seeing lots of paint!" said James Morrison. "Starting with your own bedroom."

"Da-ad."

"Ma-ax."

"Dad, please. Drive!" Megan ordered, her hand already on the door handle of the Bronco. "I can't believe I haven't seen my pony in two whole days!"

"I can't believe you haven't stopped talking in two whole days," Max grumbled. "We should've sent you in the horse trailer with Pixie and Popsicle."

"That would've been better than watching you sulk for two days," Megan retorted. "Come on, Dad! Let's park this thing."

They pulled up before a big white barn that gleamed in the late-afternoon sunlight. Megan jumped out of the Bronco almost before it had rolled to a stop. She stretched her legs, glad to be on her feet for a change.

Max was tired of riding, too, but he didn't want to leave the Bronco. At least it was familiar. He closed his eyes and wished he were back at home. He remembered the day a little more than a month ago when he and Megan had learned that they would be moving to Tennessee. Their mother was going to be the head of the orthopedics unit at the big new medical center in Memphis.

Max had been horrified at the thought of leaving the town in Connecticut where he and his sister had lived all their lives. "But, Mom," he had protested, "I don't see why you can't take care of people's bones right here in Westfield."

"There's just not much call for an orthopedic surgeon here, Max. This job is a great opportunity for me to get back into the operating room. Besides," she had said with an encouraging smile, "you might like Tennessee. The real estate agent who found our new house says it's right in the middle of horse country. The town is called Hickoryville."

"HICKville, you mean," Max had muttered under his breath.

"Max, please." His mother had put her hand on his shoulder." I know it's hard to think about leaving this place. But you and Megan are going to make lots of new friends."

"I like my old friends," he'd said, crossing his arms and looking away.

His mother had turned him around so he was facing her and waited for him to meet her gaze. When he did, his blue-gray eyes shone with anger. "Max . . ." she had sighed and smoothed his hair back with a cool hand. "Try and find a way to be positive about this, won't you?"

"Okay. I positively don't want to move." Max had growled and stomped upstairs to his room.

On the last night before the movers came, Max lay on his bed and stared at the horse show ribbons that hung from a string near the ceiling, stretching most of the way around his room. For the billionth time, he had counted them, starting with the two long championship ribbons and the one reserve champion. He had counted the eleven blue ribbons and the five red ones. Before he got to the nine yellow third-place ribbons, his eyes had become blurry with tears. He and Popsicle were up for an important award in their horse show series: the Children's Hunter High-Point Horse-and-Rider Award. There was only one more show left in the season. And now he would miss it!

He understood that his mother couldn't pass up such an important position at a brand-new medical center. But he couldn't help feeling angry at her. And at his father, for not persuading his mother to let them stay and finish the show season. Max was even mad at his twin. Megan seemed happy to be moving. All she talked about was the new barn, which she hadn't even seen yet, and the kids she was sure they were going to be best friends with in no time. Max had picked up his pillow and heaved it angrily at the open door.

"Hey, watch it!"

Megan had stood in the doorway. She had picked up the pillow and tossed it back at him as she came into his room. He had caught it and covered his head with it so she wouldn't see that he had been crying.

"Tomorrow's the big day," she had said, flopping down on the edge of his bed.

Max didn't answer her.

"Max." He had let her pull the pillow off of his head. "Aren't you even a little bit excited about moving? I mean, I know you're sad about missing the last show and all, but I just know there are going to be tons of kids at the new barn. And we'll have the whole summer to hang out with them. It could be really great!"

"Airhead," he had said scornfully to his sister. "What makes you think you'll be so popular?"

"What makes you think I won't, manure-breath? At least I'm not sitting around pouting. *I'm* going to make the best of this." She had dumped the pillow back on his head and flounced out.

"Max, come *on*. Don't you want to see Popsicle?" Megan's impatient voice shook him from his daydream. He closed his eyes tightly and wished that when he opened them he would find himself back in the driveway at their old house in Connecticut.

"Max, what are you *doing* in there? Aren't you getting out?" Megan's voice was insistent. The Bronco was already getting stuffy in the early summer heat. Max sighed and opened his eyes. The new barn stood before him, big and strange.

Slowly, he unbuckled the seat belt, opened the door, and stepped out of the back seat. His left leg had gone to sleep, and he moved it gingerly, waiting for the feeling to return, then wincing as it came back in hot prickles. He limped toward his family.

"What's the matter with your foot, Max?" his father asked him.

"My leg's asleep," he explained.

"My butt's asleep," Megan said.

"Your brain's asleep," Max countered.

Megan rolled her eyes and marched purposefully ahead of her brother. Max wished he could feel excited about this new barn, but he was too homesick even to pretend he liked it. For once, he wished he could be more like his sister. Megan never seemed to mind new situations. In fact, if she thought things weren't interesting enough, she'd make up some excitement! Though Max was more cautious, he often found himself caught up in his sister's enthusiasm. But not this time.

Megan was usually glad to have her brother as a partner in her schemes. But now, even she was tired of him. Max watched her pull open the door of the main barn and step inside without a backward glance.

2

EVEN BEFORE SHE REACHED THE DOOR, MEGAN COULD smell the horses. She stepped from the bright sunshine into the shady, cool barn and stood still, waiting for her eyes to adjust to the dim light. She could hear the sounds of the horses moving in their stalls, munching their hay, occasionally snorting and sighing. There was the knock of a metal shoe hitting wood as one horse kicked at a fly. She took a deep breath and smelled the good, familiar smell of all horse stables: the delicious scent of fresh hay mixed with the smells of clean leather, the nutty molasses smell of the feed, and the salty-sweet warmth of the horses' bodies and breath. Even the underlying smell of manure was not unpleasant, just familiar.

Megan sighed with happiness. *It's the best smell in the world,* she thought. She looked down the barn aisle at the trunks outside the stalls, which she knew contained leg wraps, brushes, and liniments for each horse. She glanced into the tack room to her left and saw rows of saddles stacked neatly on their racks, bridles hanging underneath. A few of the racks were empty. Soon she'd be hanging her own saddle on one of them.

Suddenly, she heard a familiar whinny. She hurried toward the sound. The barn formed a T shape, and as she turned right into the second aisle, Megan saw a familiar pair of gray ears above an alert pair of brown eyes looking right at her.

"Pixie! Hello, girl!" Megan quickly undid the latch and tugged on the stall door until it slid sideways. Then she slipped inside and threw her arms around her pony's neck. Pixie nuzzled at Megan's cheek with her velvety nose. Megan giggled as the pony blew hot breath into her ear. "I know what you want," she said, digging with one hand into the pocket of her shorts while she continued to hug Pixie with the other arm. She pulled out a roll of breath mints and fed one to Pixie, who chomped happily on it.

"Meg?" Max called.

"Over here," she answered, handing Pixie another mint. "In the second aisle."

Max came over and poked his head into Pixie's stall. "Boy, is she dirty," he observed. "Where's Popsicle? Did you see him?"

"He's right there." Megan pointed to the stall across from Pixie's.

When Max saw Popsicle's white face with the one blue eye looking out over the stall wall, he smiled for the second time that day. His smile quickly faded and became a frown, though, when he opened the door and saw the big cut on Popsicle's knee.

"Oh, no!" he cried.

"What's the matter?"

"I can't believe it. Just look at this!" Popsicle stepped toward Max and greeted him with a friendly nudge in the chest. Max patted him absently. He stared at Popsicle's leg, feeling more and more upset. The knee was puffy and swollen. The cut was oozing and fresh, but it had been cleaned and coated with yellow ointment.

Megan closed the door of Pixie's stall and came over to stand by Max. "Wow, what happened to him?" she asked.

"I don't know, but I'm going to find out right now," Max said firmly. He slid the door of the stall closed and marched back to the main aisle. Megan hurried behind him, hoping that he wouldn't say anything that would get them both into trouble. It took a lot to set Max off, but Megan could tell he was really angry.

Max jerked open the screen door of the little office and stepped inside. Megan was right behind him. Their parents were talking to a tall man wearing jeans and cowboy boots. The screen door closed with a bang that made Megan jump. The three adults turned around.

12

"What kind of entrance was that?" Rose Morrison frowned at her children.

Max ignored his mother. "What happened to Popsicle's knee?" he demanded, folding his arms across his chest.

"These are my children, Megan and Max," James Morrison said, giving his son a warning look. "Kids, this is the owner of Thistle Ridge Farm, Mr. Wyndham."

"Call me Jake. Every time I hear somebody say 'Mr. Wyndham,' I keep looking around for my daddy." The man smiled at them. He had thinning sandy-colored hair and bright blue eyes surrounded with creases from laughing or squinting in strong sunlight.

"That's a fine little mare you got there, Missy," Jake said to Megan. "You want to sell her?"

"NEVER!" Megan said fiercely, before she saw that Jake was only teasing.

"What happened to my horse's KNEE?" Max repeated. He was glaring at Jake.

Jake rested his hands on his hips and looked right back at Max. His face was very tan, which made his blue eyes stand out even more. "Well now, I guess he banged it up in the trailer somehow. It was like that when we went to unload him yesterday morning. I washed it and put some ointment on it."

"Stupid barn," Max muttered. "They can't even ship a horse safely!"

"Max. That will do." Rose Morrison had a quiet,

gentle voice, but when she added that tone to it, no one had better dare question her. She used the same voice in the operating room to tell her assistants what she needed. Max knew better than to say anything else after that. He shoved his hands in his pockets and scowled at the floor.

"I wouldn't worry about your gelding, son," Jake told Max. "I've seen a lot worse. It looks bad, but it's not deep. That knee'll heal up just fine. You can cold-hose it to keep the swelling down. In a week or so, you won't even know it was hurt." He gave Max's shoulder a squeeze and winked at Megan.

Megan winked back. She had decided that she liked Jake. Just then, a framed photograph on the wall behind Jake caught her eye. It was a picture of a woman jumping a very large horse over an enormous fence. The woman's expression was confident and determined, just like her horse's. Suddenly, Megan recognized the rider. Only last month, she had appeared on the cover of *Horse and Pony* magazine in her red United States Equestrian Team jacket.

Megan's mouth dropped open. She asked the grown-ups, "Is this Sharon Wyndham's farm?"

Jake chuckled. "Yeah, it's Sharon's, but the place wouldn't run if it weren't for me. Sharon's always sitting on some fancy warm-blood horse she's training for somebody-or-other. She gets all the glory, and I do all the work," he joked.

"Mom, I can't believe you didn't tell us this was

Sharon Wyndham's barn," Megan said in amazement. "Where is she? Can we meet her?"

"She's on a horse-buying trip, but she'll be back tomorrow. You'll meet her soon enough," Jake said. "Why don't you two go on outside? We've got some paperwork to finish up here."

"Okay!" Megan said. "Come on, Max." She grabbed her brother's shirtsleeve and tugged him toward the door. He let her lead him out, then headed for Popsicle's stall.

"Can you believe this is actually Sharon Wyndham's barn?" Megan was saying. "I wonder if Sharon teaches lessons. I'll bet she's too busy training for the next Olympics. Wouldn't it be cool if we could take lessons from her? Imagine telling that to the kids at our old barn!"

"Who cares?" Max said. He sat down on their tack trunk which still had the logo from their old barn in Connecticut painted on the front. He crossed his arms and kicked at the trunk with one sneakered heel.

"Poor Popsicle," Megan said, peering into his stall. She sat down on the trunk next to Max. He was staring at the concrete floor. Megan couldn't see his eyes, but she knew her brother well enough to know there might be tears in them. She'd probably feel just as bad if it were her own pony that had been injured. She tried to think of a way to make him feel better.

"Hey, Max," she said.

"What?" he answered without looking up.

15

"Let's go take a look around the place," she suggested, standing up.

"What for?" Max kicked the tack trunk again.

"Maybe we'll see some other kids." Megan sounded excited.

"We won't. It's late. Everybody's gone," Max said.

Megan was silent for a moment. Then she thought of something. "Maybe we'll see Quasar and Cuckabur, the horses Sharon Wyndham rode in the Olympics! I bet they're around here somewhere." She stood looking hopefully at Max. She knew that her brother loved Cuckabur, Sharon's big jumper.

Max thought for a moment. He would like to see Cuckabur. "Okay," he said, and got off the trunk.

They made their way down one side of the aisle, looking into each stall. They crossed another, shorter aisle. To the left were two wash stalls for bathing horses. To the right, they glimpsed a grassy area with a couple of shade trees, a picnic table, and a big stone barbecue grill.

They came to the end of the aisle and stood looking out the wide doorway. The barn sat on top of a high hill, overlooking more of the lush, hilly acres they had seen from the main road. The fences dividing the pastures were made of sturdy cedar which had weathered to a silvery gray. Several ponds glimmered in the late-afternoon sun. There were stands of trees, mostly pine and pin oak and an occasional sycamore with its smooth, spotted bark. They could just make out a small group of horses grazing near one of the ponds, almost motionless except for the constant swishing of their tails.

"It's really pretty here, isn't it?" Megan shaded her eyes as she scanned the fields.

"I guess so," said Max. He gazed at the rolling landscape. This farm was much bigger than the farm in Connecticut. "I wonder if they'll let us ride out there." He imagined cantering up that first big hill and walking along the top of it. It would be fun to ride into the woods there, ducking branches and following trails. Then he remembered Popsicle's injured knee. Every time he looked for something good about this place, something bad seemed to cancel it out.

He turned and headed back up the other side of the aisle, looking into each stall as he passed it. Megan trailed behind him, commenting on the horses and reading aloud the name plaques on each door. So far, they hadn't seen the Olympic horses.

"Cinnamon ... Newton ... Historic Holmes— weird name. Oh, I get it—like 'Homes' only it's 'Holmes—'"

"Megan." Max cut her off. "Did you happen to notice something?"

"What?" she said, stopping next to him.

"They're all horses," Max said seriously.

"So? What are you looking for, goats?" Megan started walking up the aisle.

"No," Max said. "Ponies. There are no ponies. They're all horses."

17

Megan stopped and turned around. "Oh," she said doubtfully. "Well, maybe the kids here ride horses. *You* ride a horse. I just happen to like ponies."

"It's just like I thought," Max said glumly. "This is probably a stuffy old grown-up barn. They probably only do *dressage.*"

"I sure hope not," Megan said anxiously. "I don't like to have to think about being so *correct* when I'm riding. That one time when we practiced a dressage test, I never did get Pixie to halt at X!" She looked around her. "These can't *all* be dressage horses."

"Did you see any jumps in that big outdoor ring?" Max asked her.

"Well, no, but we haven't exactly seen the whole place," Megan pointed out.

"I knew it." Max walked on, shaking his head in disgust. "No ponies, no jumps, no other kids!"

"Gosh, Max, will you quit being like that?" Megan said impatiently. "You're starting to make *me* feel down, and I don't want to! I know we're both going to love this place! Give it a chance, why don't you?"

"Megan, Max, time to go," their father called to them from the main aisle.

"Okay, Dad," Megan answered. Max ran to take a last look at Popsicle, while Megan went to Pixie's stall to give her one last pat.

"Hurry, please. I want to get to the new house

18

before it gets dark. Sometimes these country roads aren't marked very well."

Back in the Bronco, all the way to the new house, Max and Megan were both silent. Megan was thinking excitedly about having a lesson with Sharon Wyndham. For just a moment she frowned, remembering what Max had said about there being no ponies at the new barn. But she quickly dismissed it. After all, it was really late. Everyone must have gone home already. Who ever heard of a barn where there were no kids and no ponies? Megan imagined the girls she would soon meet. She wondered if they would know how to make a bracelet from braided horsehair. She imagined showing them all how. Then they would go on a trail ride. Megan smiled to herself.

Max stared out the window at the darkening countryside. He knew he ought to stop acting so glum, but he just couldn't think of anything to feel good about. He was worried about Popsicle's knee, and even more worried about the possibility that this was a grown-up barn, where he and Megan would be the only kids. He sighed. Tomorrow, he guessed, they'd find out.

3

MEGAN AND MAX HAD TO SPEND MOST OF THE NEXT DAY unpacking, sweeping, and washing windows. It was afternoon by the time their father drove them to the barn. Megan felt excited all over again as they turned up the long, tree-lined drive.

The barn was as busy today as it had been quiet the day before. Max went straight into the barn, while Megan took a look around. In the dressage ring, a woman on a big bay horse was practicing a test as someone read out instructions to her from a paper. In another ring several people were riding, while in a third ring, a small child in a large safety helmet was having a lesson on an old gray horse who trotted around in the tiniest steps imaginable while the child struggled to post.

"Walk, Willow," Megan heard the instructor tell the gray. The old horse walked. The instructor said something that made the child giggle. Megan smiled. Maybe one day she'd be a riding instructor. It would be fun to teach beginners to ride. Megan remembered how it felt to canter for the first time. And when she'd learned to jump—well, jumping Pixie was like flying. There was nothing Megan loved more than sailing around a jump course, feeling Pixie's smooth canter underneath her.

Suddenly, she was eager to see her pony. Megan went to Pixie's stall. She looked in and saw clean shavings—but no pony! Max was standing with a puzzled expression before Popsicle's empty stall.

"Max, where are they?" Megan asked.

"I don't know. Let's find Mr. Wyndham," Max said.

They headed back toward the front of the barn, looking for Jake, but he was not in the office. Just outside the office was a big bulletin board covered with notices headed "For Sale." Megan remembered that her chaps were getting too small for her. She'd see if she could put up a notice to try and sell them.

"Come on," Max said. "Let's keep looking."

"Wait." Megan grabbed his sleeve. Something on the bulletin board had caught her eye.

"What is it?"

"Look!" Megan pointed to a booklet tacked up in the middle of the bulletin board. It was a prize list, with all the classes and entry information for a horse show.

" 'Thistle Ridge Farm Year-end Awards Show,' " Max read. "It's a B-rated."

"When is it?" Megan asked.

Max read the dates. " 'Saturday and Sunday, June 7 and 8.' It's next weekend!"

"Cool! Let's look at the classes," Megan said, taking down the prize list.

They began flipping through the pages. Max slapped a page before Megan could turn it. "They have a Children's Hunter division!" he said excitedly. "Great!"

Megan was still flipping through the pages, looking for her favorite division. "Max, I can't find the Pony Jumpers," she said.

"Let me see." He took the prize list and looked through it. "I don't see it either. They have jumpers, but the fences are pretty high. It doesn't say anything about ponies."

"Oh, no," Megan moaned. "Maybe they left it out by mistake. I *hope* it's a mistake."

"Well, neither one of us is going to be riding if we don't find our horses." Max tacked the prize list back up. "Come on, Meg. Let's go ask one of the grooms."

They went down the main aisle first, being careful to stay out of everyone's way. Horses stood on cross-ties in the aisle, being groomed or tacked or having their legs wrapped. Some were just waiting while their stalls were mucked out.

"Who should we ask?" Megan whispered.

"I don't know," Max said doubtfully. "They all look so busy."

A woman came in leading a big bay horse. Megan recognized them as the pair she'd seen practicing in the dressage ring earlier. The woman's breeches were smeared with mud. The horse looked tired and sweaty.

"He's pretty," Megan said to the woman. "What's his name?"

"Mud, if he doesn't straighten up soon," the woman said angrily.

Megan put out a hand to pat the horse's neck. To her surprise, he pinned his ears and snapped at her! She jerked her hand back just in time.

"Don't touch him!" the woman snapped. "He bites people."

"I see," Megan said, embarrassed. "Sorry. I didn't know."

"You shouldn't meddle in things you know nothing about." The woman sniffed.

"Oh, I know all about horses," she told the woman. "I'm pretty experienced." She pointed to the woman's muddy breeches. "It looks like you fell off. Are you okay? At my old barn, I rode all the problem horses and ponies. I'd be glad to ride him for you anytime you need someone."

"Well! Of all the—ride *my* horse for me? How dare you speak to me like that!" the woman exclaimed.

"I-I was only offering to help," Megan stammered.

"Who is your mother?" the woman demanded. "I'm going to report you to the management! When Sharon Wyndham hears about this, you'll be banned from ever coming here again!"

"My sister didn't mean it that way," Max spoke up. "She's sorry, aren't you, Meg?" He poked her with an elbow to get her to answer.

"Yes, I'm sorry," Megan said. Under her breath, she added, "Sorry I met you."

"Me-eg!" Max hissed.

"Oh!" The woman threw the horse's reins at a groom and stormed up the aisle. The groom, a tall girl wearing cutoffs and a very dirty T-shirt, took the reins without saying a word and watched the woman until the office door slammed behind her.

Max turned to his sister. "Now you've done it! We've only been here a day, and already you've gotten us thrown out. What are we going to do? Can't you ever just keep your mouth shut?"

"Don't worry," the girl said as she slipped the horse's bridle off and replaced it with an expensive leather halter. "She can't really have you thrown out of the barn."

"If she were my owner, I'd bite people, too!" Megan said to the horse. "What a terrible woman!"

The girl chuckled. "That's Mrs. Sloane. Sharon doesn't think much of her, either, but she pays board on two stalls plus lessons and all, so she keeps her around. Actually, she and her daughter have been thrown out of nearly every other barn in the county. Nobody can stand them."

24

She clipped the cross-ties to the halter, took off the saddle, and put an anti-sweat sheet on the horse, who was still wet from his workout. Megan and Max watched her move around the horse with the assurance of someone who had been doing it all her life. She looked like someone who could persuade a horse to do anything.

"What's your names?" she asked in a thick, friendly Southern accent.

The twins introduced themselves.

"Oh, you're the new boarders. I heard you was coming. I'm Allie. Or just Al if you want."

"Allie, we're looking for our horses," Max said. "They were in the first two stalls on the second aisle, but now they're gone, and nobody seems to know where they are. Do you know? Did someone move them?"

Allie chuckled, " 'Course I know where they are. I turned 'em out myself this morning. They're down in the back paddock. Come on, I'll show you."

The twins followed her down a path wide enough for two horses to go abreast. It ran along a fence line down the hill and through a section of woods. Soon they saw a large, rectangular paddock with two very familiar shapes grazing under a shade tree in the far corner. Megan ran to the fence and called to Pixie in the special way she always called her when she was in turnout. Then she smiled expectantly, waiting for Pixie to come trotting to her just like she always did. Pixie and Popsicle raised their heads, ears pricked forward, and looked at the threesome for a moment. Then they both went back to grazing.

"Hey," Megan said, sounding dismayed. "How come she didn't pay any attention to me when I called her? She always comes when I call her. Pixie! Pixie, girl!" She tried again.

Allie chuckled. "Doesn't look like they missed you as much as you missed them." She stuck one foot on the bottom rail and rested her elbows on the fence. Megan and Max climbed up and sat perched on the top rail. The three of them watched the ponies happily munching grass.

"Do you ride, Allie?" Megan asked.

"Sure, all my life. My granddaddy set me up on ol' Big Red when I was just a little thing, and I've been riding horses ever since."

"Do you ride English?" Max asked.

"I can, but I really like Western better. The way you English riders go around, up, down, up, down . . ." She shook her head. "I never did see why folks want to stay so busy on a horse's back when you could just sit there and enjoy the ride." Allie glanced at her watch. "It's just about feeding time. Do you think you can catch these two and lead them back by yourselves?"

"Sure, Allie," Max and Megan said together.

"All right, then. Their halters are hanging on the fence there." She pointed. "Y'all be careful." She went back up the path toward the barn.

They took the halters and went to catch the horses. Max walked right up to Popsicle and slipped the halter over his head. Megan almost had a hand on Pixie, when all of a sudden the pony snorted, wheeled around, and kicked into the air not far from where Megan was standing. Then she put her head down and began to graze again.

"Watch out, Meg," Max cautioned her. "Don't get kicked."

"Here, Pixie. Here, girl." Megan slowly approached Pixie's head with an outstretched hand. "I wish I had a carrot," she muttered. Megan pulled a handful of grass and held it out to the pony. Pixie sniffed at the offering, turned her back, and trotted a little farther away.

"Why is she doing that, Max?" Megan was puzzled and angry. "I never had any trouble catching her before."

"I don't know," Max said. "Want me to try?"

"Okay, I guess." Meg went to hold Popsicle, who was quietly munching grass. She watched as Max walked slowly up to Pixie, slipped the lead line around her neck, and put on the halter. He led the captured pony toward Megan and held out the end of the lead line for her to take.

"Why did she let you catch her when she wouldn't let me come near her?" Megan asked in amazement, taking Pixie and handing Popsicle's lead line to Max.

Max shrugged. "I have no idea. Maybe you smell funny to her."

"How could I smell any different from you?"

"You ought to take a bath once in a while."

Megan scowled at him, trying to think of a come-back. Then she giggled. It was true that last night she had been too tired to take a bath. "Do you really think that could be it?"

"Who knows?" Max said. "Come on. Let's head up to the barn. I want to wash Popsicle's knee and get a good look at it."

They started toward the barn. Popsicle walked along quietly, but Pixie jigged and sidestepped all the way up the hill. She was sometimes a little frisky, but today it was taking all of Megan's concentration just to lead her safely. She jerked the lead line for the hundredth time. "Pixie!" she said sternly. "Be-have!"

The pony walked for three strides, balked, then began prancing again. "Why is she so nervous?" Megan wondered.

Just then, Pixie froze. Three deer came bounding across the path, not ten yards in front of them. Pixie's eyes grew wild. She snorted, then reared, nearly jerking Megan off her feet.

"Meg, let go of the lead line!" Max yelled.

She did as he said, and Pixie bolted for the barn. Megan took off after her. "Oh, no!" she cried out as she imagined her frightened pony galloping all the way through the busy barn. She put on a burst of speed and tore up the hill as fast as she could go, hoping Pixie hadn't caused any damage.

Megan was gasping by the time she reached the top of the hill. She staggered into the barn, looking for Pixie. She was relieved to see that the pony hadn't run all the way down the aisle. Pixie stood trembling, as a boy about Megan's size came toward the frightened mare. He spoke softly as he slowly put out a hand and patted her neck. She flinched as he touched her, but she stood still. Then the boy bent to pick up the end of the lead line that trailed between Pixie's legs.

Megan rested with her hands on her knees, trying to catch her breath. She told herself it was from the hard run, but her heart was pounding from the scare she'd had when Pixie reared. "Thanks for catching her," she told the boy when she could speak.

"You're welcome," he said, handing her the lead line. He was a little taller than Megan, with darkly tanned skin, longish, shiny black hair, and dark, sparkling eyes. "What spooked her?" he asked.

"I think it was the deer. There were three of them. They just came charging across the path, right in front of us. She was acting funny when I went to catch her. I guess she must've smelled them."

"I never saw a horse spook at a deer. There are so many around here, they're all just used to it," the boy told her.

"Well, I guess Pixie's never seen one until now," Megan said.

Max came into the barn leading Popsicle. The boy stared at them. "Hey! Is that your horse?" he said. He was staring at Popsicle.

"Yes," Max said proudly.

29

"Your horse looks just like my horse!" the boy exclaimed. "Except Penny hasn't got a blue eye. But they're the same color, and they even have the same white markings—four white stockings and a blaze face."

Max watched the boy, who slowly circled Popsicle, examining him critically as he spoke. Now he stood right by Max. Max wasn't sure if the boy was being friendly or getting ready to start a fight.

"I'm Max Morrison," Max tried. "What's your name?"

"Keith Bradley Hill. Pleased to meet you." The boy smiled and shook hands with Max. Max smiled back, relieved that he wasn't going to have to defend himself or his horse.

"I'm Megan Morrison," said Megan.

Keith ignored her. "You want to see my mare? You won't believe it, I swear, they look *just alike!*"

"Sure," Max said. "Where is she?"

"This way," Keith said.

Megan watched the boys walk right past her as if she had disappeared. She spoke to her pony. "Well, Pixie, would you like to see the horse that looks just like Popsicle?" She gently nodded Pixie's head up and down by the halter. "You would? So would I."

Just then, a loud whinny came from the stall beside Pixie's. It startled all of them. A white face with two liquid brown eyes and two pretty chestnut ears was pressed eagerly against the bars that enclosed the top of the stall.

Popsicle's ears went up. His head went up. His whole body quivered as he let loose a long, loud whinny in reply. Then he dragged Max down the aisle, stretched his neck as far as he could, and pushed his nose against the bars. The two horses blew air into each other's nostrils, snorted, then both whinnied again. The kids all burst out laughing.

"It's like they're looking in a mirror at each other!" Max said.

"I think Penny's in love." Keith laughed.

Megan put Pixie in her stall and stood watching the two horses. They really did seem love-struck. Max had a hard time getting Popsicle away from Penny. At last, he gave a mighty tug and managed to get his head turned away.

"I need to cold-hose Popsicle's knee," Max said to Keith. "Want to come?"

"Sure," Keith said. "The wash stalls are over here."

Megan watched the two boys head for the wash stall, chattering away as if they were already best friends. She started to follow them but then stopped. They hadn't asked her to come along. She shoved her hands into the pockets of her shorts and went back to Pixie's stall, feeling a little left out. She opened the door and fed Pixie a breath mint.

"Sorry, girl, but that's the last one. I'll get some more on the way home tonight." She scratched

Pixie gently behind her ears. Pixie closed her eyes with pleasure and lowered her head. Suddenly, Pixie jerked her head up, her eyes open wide. At the same time, Megan heard a sound that sent chills up her spine in spite of the warm day. Someone was screaming!

4

THE BLOODCURDLING SHRIEKS WERE COMING FROM THE direction of the main aisle. Megan dashed toward the sound. She hurried around the corner and stopped, trying to see what might be wrong.

The screaming had stopped. Now there was only a low, moaning sound. Megan saw a girl about her size standing beside a white pony. It was the girl who was making the noise, but Megan couldn't see what was the matter.

"Are you okay?" she asked doubtfully.

The girl looked up and began to wail. Her eyes pleaded with Megan, but she didn't speak. Megan felt growing alarm. "What's wrong?" she asked her.

The girl lurched her head and shoulders away from the pony several times in a row. Then she moaned again. The pony stood calmly beside her.

"How—can—I—help—you?" Megan said, very

slowly and loudly. She had started to think that perhaps the girl was hearing-impaired. She hoped she could read lips.

The girl closed her eyes as if she were in great pain. She pointed at the ground.

Megan looked where she pointed and saw that the girl had dropped the pony's reins. Was she unable to bend down to pick them up? "You want me to pick up the reins for you?" Megan asked doubtfully.

"Oooooooooh . . ." the girl groaned.

Megan picked up the reins so the pony wouldn't step in them. Just then, the pony picked up his right hind leg to rest it and shifted his weight onto his left front foot. The girl began to scream again.

"What is it? What's the matter? Please tell me, and I'll help you!" Megan begged the distressed girl. Again, the girl moaned and began pointing frantically toward the ground. Megan looked anxiously all around. She couldn't tell what the girl was pointing at. Then she saw what the trouble was. The pony was standing on the girl's foot!

Megan put her own shoulder against the pony's and shoved. The pony moved aside obediently. The girl sat down abruptly, right on the barn floor, and stared at her foot with a horrified expression. "Oooooh, my tooooooe," she wailed pitifully.

Megan squatted down next to the girl. "Let's take off your boot and see how it looks," she suggested.

"Okay." The girl sniffed.

Megan was relieved that the girl could talk after

all and didn't seem to have anything more seriously wrong with her than a squashed toe. She reached for the girl's bootlace. To her surprise, the girl screamed again and jerked her foot away.

"Don't touch it!" she said.

"Well, I know it must hurt," Megan said, "but we ought to look at it, in case you really broke it or something."

"All right," the girl said warily.

Again, Megan reached for the girl's foot. "No!" she yelled, and jerked her foot away.

Megan sighed in frustration. "What's your name?"

"Amanda."

"Amanda, listen. Reach down and untie your boot, okay?"

Amanda gingerly untied the knot and began to loosen the laces, wincing in an exaggerated way with each tiny tug. Megan felt herself growing impatient. She had been stepped on by horses many times. It hurt a lot, but her riding boots had protected her from getting anything more than a bad bruise.

At last, the laces were undone. Amanda let Megan help her slide the boot off, then pulled off her sock. Both girls bent to examine the foot. A red spot under her toenail was starting to turn bluish.

"Do you think it's broken?" Amanda asked.

"If you have to ask me, probably not," Megan told her. "A horse smashed my toe once, stomping at a fly. It looked just like that."

"What happened to it? Was it broken?"

Megan shook her head. "No. But my toenail turned blue, and half of it came off. But it grew back!" Megan hastily reassured her. Amanda had looked as if she might scream again.

Amanda sat back with her arms spread behind her and surveyed her toe suspiciously. "Do you think I can ride with an injury like this?" she said, never taking her eye off her own foot.

"I don't know. Put your boot on again and see how it feels."

"I bet I can't possibly ride with this toe. I bet it's fractured. It feels like it's fractured. How can I possibly ride with a fractured toe? I can't, can I?" Amanda sounded curiously satisfied. "I'll just have to drop out of the horse show. Oh, dear. What a shame." Amanda gave a long, exaggerated sigh, but Megan thought she sounded glad.

"Which horse show?" Megan asked.

"Why, the Thistle Ridge Farm Year-end Awards Show," Amanda replied. "Don't you know anything?"

"I just moved here," Megan explained. "But I saw the prize list on the bulletin board. I thought that was the show you were talking about. Are you up for any awards?"

"Well, of *course* I am," Amanda said coldly. "Don't you *know* who I *am*? Don't you know who my *pony* is?"

"I guess not. Is this him?" Megan gestured to the pony whose reins she was still holding.

"Of course it's my pony," Amanda said haughtily. "This is Jump for Joy." She announced it as if she expected Megan to react with awe.

"He's pretty," Megan said politely. Jump for Joy put out his dainty white muzzle and licked Megan's arm. Megan smiled and scratched his face under the cheek pieces of the bridle. He half closed his eyes with pleasure, enjoying the attention.

"Pretty? *Pretty?*" Amanda scoffed. "He's more than just pretty. He's perfect. He cost twenty thousand dollars, and he's twelve years old. He does fourth-level dressage. Do you know what *dressage* is?"

"I know what dressage is," Megan said. "What award are you up for?"

"Pony Hunter Champion of the Year," Amanda said smugly. "I only need one more blue ribbon to put me over the top. And I'm sure to win it in this show."

"I thought you said you weren't going to ride because of your toe," Megan reminded her.

"Oh, I guess I'll just have to suffer with it. I can't disappoint everyone, can I?" The girl stared at her bruised toe, turning her foot so she could study it from different angles.

"I guess not. My name is Megan." She tried out her friendliest smile on Amanda. "It's nice to finally meet another kid my age."

Amanda looked up at Megan. It was the first time she had seemed interested in anything except herself. She was about to speak, when they both heard someone calling.

"Mandy? Mandy! Is that you? Amanda Susannah Sloane, you get off that dirty barn floor this *instant!* I didn't buy you those expensive jodhpurs to have you ruin them like that. Get *up!*"

It was Mrs. Sloane, the woman with the big bay horse that bit at everyone. Megan realized that she must be Amanda's mother. She was wearing clean white breeches and a pink riding shirt with a monogrammed collar. She held a long dressage whip in one hand. As she stopped in front of the two girls, she tapped her whip impatiently on the side of her boots.

Amanda instantly began to whine again. "Mama, Jump for Joy stepped on my foot, and he wouldn't get off. It's fractured, I just know it is. We need to call an ambulance right away." Amanda buried her face in her hands and wept.

"What are you doing with my daughter's pony?" Mrs. Sloane demanded. "This is all *your* fault, isn't it? I knew the minute I saw you that you were a troublemaker." She stepped toward Megan. "I'll not have you around my daughter, causing her personal injury. Now, you just *hand me those reins.*" She smacked the whip against her boot in time with the words. The pony squinted his eyes and cringed as if he expected she was going to hit him.

Megan was completely astonished. She didn't know what to say. Wordlessly, she held out the reins to Mrs. Sloane. Amanda had stopped wailing to watch with interest while her mother picked on Megan, but she began to whimper again as soon as her mother's attention shifted to her.

"Mama, I just don't see how I can possibly be well enough to show on Saturday," she whined.

"Amandasusloane, yes you will." She said Amanda's whole name as if it were one word. "You will put on your boot this minute and march yourself right on down to that ring for your lesson."

"But, Mama, my toe really hurts. I just don't think I can put my boot on," Amanda protested.

"Then *I* will put it on *for* you," Mrs. Sloane announced. She bent down and began stuffing Amanda's foot back into her paddock boot, while Amanda squirmed and yelled. Mrs. Sloane was still holding the end of Jump for Joy's reins and kept jerking the bit in his mouth each time she yanked on Amanda's foot. The poor pony suffered patiently. Megan wanted to offer to hold the pony, but she was afraid to say anything.

"Now, you get up and take this pony, and go down to the ring and be warmed up by the time Sharon gets down there." Mrs. Sloane glared at her watch, which was studded with diamonds sparkling in the light from the door. "You have exactly twelve minutes." She held out the reins to Amanda. Megan watched them dangling from the end of Mrs. Sloane's bright pink fingernails. They were beautiful braided reins, the most expensive kind. Any rider would love to have reins like that.

Amanda got up without even bothering to dust

off her seat. Bits of hay clung to the back of her jodhpurs. She took the reins sullenly, muttering, "I can't ride with this toe. I just know it is fractured. I will never be able to ride in the horse show. We'll have to scratch."

"We will do no such thing." Amanda's mother planted her hands on her hips. "I didn't pay twenty thousand dollars for this pony and make sure you rode in every single show this year to have you miss the most important one of the whole season. You are going to ride on Saturday if your toe falls right off your foot."

"It feels like it's falling off right now," Amanda complained.

"Then Daddy and I will buy you a new one." Mrs. Sloane smiled brightly, without an ounce of kindness or good humor. Amanda limped out the door, dragging the pony along behind her. She held the reins under his chin but hadn't bothered to pick up the ends, which dragged in the dust. How the pony managed not to step in them, Megan didn't know.

"I just know it's fractured," Megan heard her grumbling again.

Then Mrs. Sloane must have thought of something else to tell Amanda because she hurried out the door after her. Megan breathed a sigh of relief. "That poor pony," she said to herself. Then she went to find Max.

The boys were in the wash stall, laughing and talking while Max let the hose run on Popsicle's knee.

"You guys, you'll never believe what just happened." Megan started to explain how she'd met Amanda Sloane, but Keith interrupted her.

"Yeah, everybody knows what a pain she is," Keith said. "Hey, Max, you want to go on a trail ride tomorrow morning? I could show you the whole place. Did you know Thistle Ridge is about a hundred and seventy acres?"

"Wow. Oh, yeah! I mean, if Popsicle's leg is okay . . ." Max frowned, then brightened. "Hey, Meg, could I ride Pixie if it's not? You don't mind, do you?"

Megan's mouth dropped open. Would Max really take Pixie and not even consider inviting her along? She was trying to think what to say, when Jake Wyndham came strolling toward them.

"Hey, Jake!" Keith said, his face lighting up.

"Hey there, Keith. Megan, Max." He was wearing a faded Atlanta Braves baseball cap. He lifted the cap and wiped his sweaty forehead. "Max, can I borrow that hose for just a second?" He stooped and took a long drink of water, then handed the hose back to Max.

"Jake, do you think I can ride Popsicle tomorrow? Keith said he would take me on a trail ride."

"I don't see why you can't ride him. Just take it easy the first couple of days." Jake winked at Max and went back to the office.

Keith grinned at Max. He put out a hand, and Max slapped at it. "All right! Trail ride tomorrow A.M.! What time can you get here?"

"I'll ask my dad. He's coming to pick us up soon."
Max glanced down the aisle toward the door.

"Cool! Hey, why don't you give me your phone
number and we can plan it tonight?" Keith said.

"What about me? Can I come on the trail ride,
too?" Megan asked.

The boys didn't seem to hear her. They went on
talking as if she weren't even there.

"There's this big lake I want to show you. And
we can pack a lunch to take with us. I know this
really great place up on one of the ridges where we
can stop and eat it," Keith said.

"Max." Megan waited for him to answer. "Max!"

"What?" Max shifted his attention to his twin.

"I want to come on the trail ride, too, okay?"
Megan said.

Max and Keith looked at each other. Keith
shrugged.

"I guess so," Max said.

"Good," Megan said. But she didn't really feel
very happy. "Good for *you*," she muttered, looking
at Max. "When am *I* going to make a friend?" She
left the boys in the wash stall and went outside to
wait for her father to pick them up.

5

THE NEXT DAY, MAX AND MEGAN WERE UP EARLY AND at the barn by eight o'clock. They quickly groomed and tacked their horses. Keith had put a Western saddle and bridle on Penny. He even had saddle-bags for them to pack their lunches in.

As they were heading out the door, Allie stopped them. "Hold on, you three."

"What's the matter, Allie?"

"I spoke to Jake early this morning. He told me y'all were going on a trail ride. I want to check your tack before you go."

They waited while she looked over each horse, checking to see that the saddle pads were smoothed down so there would be no wrinkles to rub sores. She picked up all twelve feet to be sure that they were free of rocks that could bruise the sensitive "frog" in the middle of the hoof. She felt under their bellies and everywhere the tack touched them to be sure no dried sweat or dirt was left where it could cause chafing. She made sure each bit hung correctly in each mouth, not too tight or too loose. Last, she checked all the girths.

"Keith, you've got to learn to get this cinch tighter," she chided him. "One of these days, your saddle's gonna come right off, and you along with it."

"She puffs her belly up, Allie," Keith protested. "I tried three times. Besides, I don't think she likes it so tight." He watched Penny pin her ears back in annoyance as Allie pulled the cinch snug.

"She won't like it any better if she gets sores rubbed on her belly from you riding with it so loose. Make sure you get me or Jake or one of the other grooms to check it for you till you learn to do it better. I mean it now, Keith," she warned him. She had caught him rolling his eyes at Max as if he thought she ought to mind her own business.

"OKAY, Allie. Now can we go?" Keith said impatiently. "It'll be dark before you even let us out the door."

"Go on. And remember to close all the gates you open."

"We will."

"And be careful."

"We WILL!"

They mounted up and started down the hill in single file. Keith led the way on Penny, followed by Max. Megan came last. Pixie was already acting nervous. Megan could feel the little mare's heart beating fast. She hoped this wasn't going to be a disaster.

For a while, Megan had her hands full trying to keep Pixie at a walk. She pranced and jigged her way down the trail, tossing her head impatiently every time Megan tried to slow her down. But when they came out of the woods into a level bottom, Pixie seemed to calm down. She gave a huge, relieved-sounding snort, put her head down, and marched along behind Popsicle and Penny, who by now were walking happily abreast.

"How old are you?" Max asked Keith.

"Ten," Keith said. "How about you?"

"Eleven," Max said.

"We both are," Megan said.

"How can you be the same age? I thought she was your sister." Keith looked puzzled.

"We're twins," Max told him.

Keith frowned. "You don't look anything alike. Your hair and eyes are different, and she's a lot shorter than you."

"But I'm older than he is," Megan said quickly.

"Age before beauty," Max countered.

"But you just said you were the same age," Keith said.

"She's older by twenty minutes," Max said.

"A day," Megan said.

"I was born twenty minutes after she was, but by then it was after midnight, so actually our birthdays are on different days," Max explained. "My mom always says we're so different, she doesn't know why we bothered to be twins."

"Well, I guess we're alike in one way," Megan said.

"What's that?" Keith asked, puzzled.

She grinned. "We both love to ride."

For a while, they rode along quietly. Max was feeling happy for the first time in a long while. He had forgotten how much he enjoyed just being on his horse, feeling the familiar rhythm of Popsicle's walk underneath him. Maybe his sister had been right. Maybe this barn would turn out to be an okay place after all. He reached forward and scratched Popsicle on his withers, just in front of the saddle.

"Why do you call him Popsicle?" Keith asked.

"Once, when I first got him," Max said, "I was standing beside him eating a Popsicle, and he reached right over and took a big bite. He's loved them ever since. You ought to see him—he takes a bite and then sticks his lips out and closes his eyes and chomps and slurps like this." Max demonstrated. "It's so funny."

"What's his favorite flavor?"

"He seems to like cherry the best, but I've never seen him turn down any flavor."

Keith laughed. "I wonder if Penny likes Popsicles. I'll have to get her one and see."

"Pixie likes breath mints," Megan told him. Neither of the boys answered her.

They walked through the bottom toward a big

hill. It was still early in the summer, but the grass was already as high as a pony's knees. Spiky purplish flowers with stickers on their deep green leaves grew everywhere.

"Those must be thistles," Megan said.

"They are thistles," Keith agreed. "And don't ever fall off on one. I did once, and, boy, did it hurt."

"How'd you fall off?" Max asked.

Keith shrugged and grinned. "My cinch was loose."

Max and Megan laughed.

"But don't tell Allie. Nobody knows except my sister, and I made her promise not to tell."

"You have a sister?" Megan perked up at the thought. "Does she ride?"

"Yeah, Penny used to be hers. She used to show her until she outgrew her. Now she's mine, aren't you, ol' girl?" He patted the mare's rump affectionately.

"You mean Penny goes English, too?"

"Penny does it all," Keith said.

"Do you show?" Max asked.

"Yeah, I do the trail classes and Western pleasure. But I love barrel racing the best! Penny loves it, too."

"Do you jump?" Max wanted to know.

Keith hesitated. "Yeaaah . . . some. I've tried it. I sort of like it—I need to practice more. Do you?"

"Oh, yes." Max told him about being up for the year-end award in the Children's Hunter division back in Connecticut.

"Oh, man, you must've been so bummed when you had to move," Keith said.

"I was." Max nodded. "I was so mad at my parents."

"I would have been, too," Keith sympathized. "Moving's the worst. I know how it is. We just moved here a year ago. Both of my parents are professors at the university in Memphis. I hated to leave my friends in Texas."

"Moving's the pits," Max said.

"I didn't mind it so much," Megan said, trying to stay in the conversation. "I miss my old friends, of course, but I'm sure I'll make lots of new ones."

"Yeah, just like you made friends with Amanda Sloane yesterday," Max said. He and Keith exchanged knowing looks.

Megan ignored him. "How old is your sister, Keith?"

"Haley? She's fourteen." Keith made a face. "She thinks she's so cool because she trains with Sharon Wyndham."

"What kind of horse does she have?" Megan asked.

"Do you think we could meet her?" Max asked at the same time.

"Haley?" Keith sounded incredulous. "What for?"

"Not Haley!" Max laughed. "I meant Sharon Wyndham!"

"Oh!" Keith laughed and shook his head. "I was wondering. Sure, you could meet her. She's nice. She's always so busy, though. If she's not riding

48

one of her own horses, she's training someone else's. Or teaching. Or mucking stalls. I don't think I've ever seen her just sit and do nothing."

They walked on, the boys in the lead, Megan following behind. They had come to the top of a big hill. From there, they could see the back of the main barn. Keith pointed to a large building off to one side. "That's the big indoor arena. Just beyond it is the little indoor ring. You saw the outdoor rings, didn't you?"

"I did," Megan said. "But I didn't see any jumps."

"That's because they're all taken down right now. They're being painted and repaired for the show. It's Thistle Ridge's big year-end awards show."

"We saw the prize list on the bulletin board," Max said. "Are you going to be in it?"

"Yeah, I guess. I'll probably take Penny in the Short Stirrup division." Keith made a face.

"What's wrong with that?" Max asked.

"I don't like the equitation divisions so much. Especially the twelve-and-under. The last time I rode in Short Stirrup, I got beaten by a six-year-old."

Max laughed. "You're kidding!"

"Nope." Keith shook his head.

"I know what you mean about equitation," Megan said. "You always feel stiff, like you can't move an inch. I like the jumpers. Then I don't have to worry about my form. I just have to be sure we get around without knocking down any rails."

"I like equitation," Max said.

"Well, you're so good at it, it's no wonder,"

Megan said. "He always used to win the Short Stirrup divisions at our schooling shows in Connecticut," she explained to Keith.

"You guys, look." Max was pointing toward the highway. A large green horse van was chugging toward the barn. It slowed and turned in at the front entrance, then vanished behind the hill.

"Is that Sharon Wyndham?" Megan asked, trying not to sound as excited as she felt.

"That's her," Keith said. "Let's go on. I want to show you the back pasture and the lake."

The three children guided their horses down the hill. Keith took them through another wooded section where the trail was so narrow, they had to bend forward and keep their heads down to avoid the branches. They came out into another pasture.

"What's that noise?" Max asked. A knocking sound came from somewhere nearby.

"Sounds like hammering," Keith said. "It must be Jake." They began looking around for him. Keith spotted him near an overgrown hedge of brambles, pounding nails into a new fence rail. His old blue Ford pickup truck was parked nearby. In the back were more cedar posts and rails and a post-hole digger.

"Hey, Jake," Keith called as soon as they were close enough.

Jake paused and looked up to see who had called him. He waved at them as they rode past, then turned back to his work.

"This way," Keith said, leading them along the

fence. Soon they came up another hill, not quite as high as the first one. From there, they could see a large lake, partly surrounded by thick pine woods.

"Ooh, isn't that pretty!" Megan exclaimed. "How do we get over there?"

"We go through the gate," Keith said, pointing to the large metal gate at the corner of the fence.

"I'll open it," Max said, starting to dismount.

"Hold on," Keith told him. "Nobody has to get off. Penny and I can open it."

The twins watched as Keith maneuvered Penny to a spot where he could lean over and unhook the chain that held the gate closed. Then he put a hand on the gate and walked Penny forward, opening the gate as they went.

"That's really cool, Keith," Max said with admiration.

"We practice it for trail classes," Keith said.

"I don't see what's so great about it," Megan muttered under her breath. She was getting really tired of Max going on and on about how great and wonderful Keith was. All the way home yesterday, all he'd talked about was his great new friend, Keith, and how cool this trail ride was going to be. Megan didn't see what was so marvelous about opening a gate. So Keith could steer his horse. Big deal.

"Will you show me how to do that?" Max asked.

"Sure, it's not that hard. It just takes patience and practice. But it's easier than having to get off your horse every time you want to open a gate."

"Well, I know a better way," Megan said. She was tired of just walking and listening to the boys go on as if she weren't there.

"What do you mean?" Max asked.

Megan was eyeing a section of fence near the gate. The top rail had come down, and the middle rail lay at an angle with one end on the ground. It would be easy to jump over the low side. "Watch this," she said.

"Meg, you know you're not supposed to be jumping without supervision," Max warned.

"You and Keith can supervise me." Megan walked Pixie several yards away from the fence, then turned around and began trotting toward the rails. She would show them some real riding. Anybody could open a stupid gate.

"Megan, don't. It's dangerous to jump without an adult watching you," Max said.

"Stop worrying so much, Max. What could possibly be dangerous about this little tiny fence?" Megan said as Pixie tucked her knees underneath her and neatly cleared the rail. "See? It's easy. Pixie loves jumps like this." Megan faced the boys and patted the mare's smooth neck. Pixie's ears were forward, and she had begun to prance in place. "She wants to do it again," Megan said.

"Well, don't," Max said.

"You can't tell me what to do," Megan retorted. She started to trot toward the fence again.

"Megan, cut it out!" Max demanded.

"Make me," she said loftily.

Pixie broke into a canter. Megan was only a few strides from the fence. At that moment, there was a crashing sound from the trees on her left. "Uh-oh," Megan said, feeling her heart sink into her stomach.

"Oh, no!" Max exclaimed. "Not again!"

6

OUT OF THE CORNER OF HER EYE, MEGAN SAW A DEER break cover and run out of the woods right behind Pixie. Pixie saw it, too, because in the next second, she doubled her strides, cleared the fence, and bolted toward the barn.

Megan saw that Max was yelling something at her, but she couldn't hear what. She knew she was galloping very fast, but she felt as if she were in a dream—one of those unpleasant ones where you are trying to get away from something dreadful but you feel as if you are dragging your arms and legs through very deep water and everything is moving in slow motion.

She glanced down and saw the ground whipping by under Pixie's flying legs. She had already left Max and Keith far behind. She flashed past Jake's blue truck and saw him drop his hammer and run

for the cab. For a second, she felt absolutely terrified. But then she realized that as long as she was
still on Pixie's back, the next thing to do was try
to stop.

She took a deep breath, sat up as much as she
dared, and gave a firm pull on both reins. "Whoa!"
she commanded. But Pixie only ran faster. Megan
shortened her reins and tried working the bit left
to right in the pony's mouth. But there was no re-
sponse. Megan realized that in her fright, the pony
must have grabbed the bit in her teeth and locked
her jaw muscles. Without the bit in place against
the bars of her mouth, Pixie wouldn't feel much of
anything Megan did with the reins.

Now they were headed for the woods they had
walked through earlier. Megan had just enough
time to grab a handful of mane and duck before
they were galloping through the trees. She didn't
dare raise her head, but she felt branches scraping
her safety helmet. She could feel Pixie changing
leads every time there was a turn in the path. Then
they were out of the woods again.

Megan was getting tired. She realized she'd had
her eyes shut when they were galloping through
the woods. She opened them now and recognized
the paddock where Pixie and Popsicle had been
turned out. Pixie was headed right for the paddock
fence. Megan thought it might stop her, but then
she realized that Pixie only saw the barn up the
hill beyond it. She was going to jump the fence!

Megan sat up one more time and gave a last desperate yank on the reins. But her arms felt weak, and her legs were beginning to tremble. Pixie didn't slow down at all. The paddock fence loomed before her. The top rail was at least four feet high. Megan bent forward into jumping position, shoved her heels down, and grabbed mane.

Pixie sailed over the fence, crossed the paddock in several strides, and jumped out. Megan managed to stay on, although she had never jumped a fence that high in her life. They were almost to the top of the hill. Megan realized that if she didn't stop, Pixie would surely gallop right down the barn aisle and maybe hurt someone.

A pretty young woman with a blond ponytail was standing at the barn door, waving her arms and shouting. Allie was standing next to her, an alarmed look on her face. "PULLEY REIN!" the blond woman yelled.

Then Megan remembered. She grabbed mane with one hand and sat back. With her other hand, she yanked the rein up and back as hard as she could several times in a row. To her relief, she felt Pixie slow down. She repeated it, and Pixie trotted. Just before they reached the barn door, Allie grabbed one of the reins and pulled Pixie to a halt.

All during the terrifying bolt, the only thing Megan could hear was the sound of Pixie's feet drumming the earth. Now that she had stopped, everything seemed so quiet. Then Megan realized she could hear her own heart pounding louder and louder. She had hung on all that time, but now she felt herself slipping out of the saddle. She tried to hold her head up, to hold on, but she had no strength left. She wondered if she might be fainting.

"Are you okay?" The blond woman was by her side, supporting her. Megan tried to speak, but no words would come out. She gulped and nodded. "I'm going to help you down," the woman said.

Jake drove up and skidded to a stop. He jumped from the truck and ran to help Megan sit down. She leaned against the barn, grateful that she no longer had to stay on her pony. It was the first time she could ever remember being glad to get off a horse.

"Is Pixie okay?" she asked.

"She'll be all right." The blond woman said. "Allie's taking care of her. How do you feel? Better?"

Megan nodded. The roaring in her ears had faded. Now that the scare was over, she was feeling more embarrassed than anything. "Where are Max and Keith?"

"I plumb forgot about those two," said Jake. "Sharon, you stay with her. I'll drive back out there and be sure they're okay."

Megan looked up at the blond woman. "Are you Sharon Wyndham?" she asked softly, dreading the answer.

"Yes. And you are?" Sharon's voice was equally soft.

"Megan Morrison," she managed to answer, feeling the words stick in her throat. For years she had dreamed of meeting this great equestrian, and now her first encounter had to be like this. What a disaster! Megan's chest ached from the tears that were beginning to fill her eyes. She was used to feeling confident and capable on any horse or pony; she'd never been in a situation where she couldn't stop a horse. And now Sharon Wyndham's first impression of her and her pony was of the two of them dashing across the farm out of control. She had been trying not to blink, but the tears began to fall anyway.

"That was some ride your pony gave you, huh?" Sharon smiled encouragingly.

Megan just nodded miserably. She couldn't speak. She was too embarrassed even to look up. She watched dejectedly as another tear splashed on her thigh, leaving a dark spot on the suede of her chaps.

"You know," Sharon continued, "when I happened to look up and see you galloping straight for the paddock fence, I thought, 'Oh, no, this kid's a goner.' I never thought you'd stay on. You're a great little rider, you know that?"

Megan could hardly believe what she was hearing. She listened intently as Sharon went on.

"Then when I saw the pony clear that fence, I couldn't believe my own eyes. That's a talented little jumper you have there."

"Thanks," Megan finally made herself answer. She explained how the deer had spooked Pixie the day before, and how they'd come across another deer in the back pasture. She started to leave out the fact that she had been jumping but decided it would be better to tell the whole truth. Sharon listened to the story without commenting.

"So, after I tried everything I could think of to stop her, and nothing worked, I decided just to try to stay on. I don't know why I didn't remember the pulley rein," Megan said sheepishly.

"It's really hard to stay calm and remember what to do in a situation like that," Sharon said. "It sounds like you did just fine. And the good thing about making it through an incident like that is that if it ever happens again, you'll remember what to do. And it will never seem as scary."

"Should I have jumped off her?" Megan asked.

"No, you did the right thing." Sharon smiled at her. "I always tell my students, 'I've never been hurt when I was *on* a horse.'"

Megan wiped her eyes and looked gratefully at Sharon. She was relieved that Sharon didn't sound angry at her, but she still wished she could simply erase the whole day and start over again.

"But jumping without your trainer, or some kind of supervision, is a really dangerous thing to do." Sharon spoke sternly. "And I think you knew that, which makes it even worse."

"I'm very sorry. I won't ever do it again," Megan said. She was as sincerely sorry as she had ever been for anything. She hoped she sounded that way.

"Feel like you could get up now?" Sharon asked.

Megan nodded. Sharon put out a hand and helped her up. Her legs still felt shaky. She brushed off the seat of her pants.

"Sharon?" Megan said.

"Yes?" Sharon looked straight at her.

"I was just wondering . . ." Megan took a deep breath. "Max and I were looking at the prize list for the horse show, and . . ."

"And what?" Sharon prompted. She glanced at her watch.

"There's no Pony Jumper division in the show," Megan said in a rush. "That's what I always show Pixie in. She's so quick, and she really loves to jump, and I'm not so great at equitating. Why don't you put in a Pony Jumper division?"

Sharon didn't move, except for one eyebrow. It shot up so far, Megan thought it might get lost in Sharon's blond hair. Then she said, "The kids I see in the Pony Jumpers are mostly just like you: talented riders with sloppy form who just like the speed and the jumps. I don't have a Pony Jumper division in my shows for exactly that reason. I think kids your age need to be doing simple courses and working on their equitation. You have to learn to ride a rhythmic canter before you're ready for the jumpers. And you seem to need a little work in that area." Sharon gave her the one high eyebrow again.

Megan got the message. "Oh. Right. Of course." She nodded fiercely, as if she had always said the same thing. Behind her back, she was wringing her hands, feeling completely overcome with embarrassment.

"Anything else?" Sharon asked.

Megan hesitated. "Well, I was just . . . My brother and I . . . We were just wondering if you might have time to give us a lesson anytime this week."

Sharon gave her the "Are you really asking me this question?" look that was going to become very familiar. Megan shifted her weight nervously and dug one toe into the dirt. Max was always telling her she didn't know when to be quiet. She wished he'd been there to elbow her before she could ask such a dumb question. Sharon was an *Olympic rider*. Why would she have time to work with some kid with "sloppy form"?

To Megan's surprise, Sharon said graciously, "I would be delighted."

"Oh! Really? Oh, that's great! That's just great! Thank you so much!" Megan backed away, beaming with happiness. A lesson with Sharon Wyndham! Maybe Sharon would even coach them in the horse show! She couldn't wait to tell Max.

She was practically skipping as she went off to look for Allie and Pixie. When Megan saw her pony, though, her heart sank right to her toes. Pixie wasn't hot or breathing heavily anymore, but she was still wet. Her dark skin showed through under her sweaty coat. She walked along wearily, her head drooping.

Megan listened carefully to Allie's instructions about how to cool the pony down. Then she took

61

the lead line and began walking slowly up and down the driveway. When they reached the top of the driveway, Megan led her to the trough for a sip of water. The pony slurped gratefully at it. Megan had to tug hard to get her away from it.

Why hadn't Max and Keith come back yet? She shaded her eyes with one hand and scanned the hills, but there was no sign of them. She remembered how Max and Keith had made her feel so left out. She'd jumped that fence even though she knew better, partly out of boredom and partly to show off. She'd wanted them to pay attention to her. Now she was sorry she'd done such a dangerous thing, but she still felt jealous of the two boys.

Megan finished walking Pixie and brought her into the barn. She pulled a stiff brush from her grooming kit and went to work. Pixie nosed at her pocket, searching for a treat. Suddenly, Megan felt angry. She pushed Pixie's nose away roughly and began to brush with hard, angry strokes. Pixie had never behaved so badly, not even at the show where somebody's car backfired loudly just as she was jumping the first fence. Megan felt as if Pixie had betrayed her.

Pixie's coat had dried into stiff spikes. Dried sweat striped her flanks in lines of white salt. Megan had never seen her look so bedraggled. Then she remembered that the whole thing might have been avoided if she hadn't jumped that fence. The more she worked on brushing Pixie clean, the more she began to blame herself for allowing such a thing to happen to her beloved pony.

"I'm sorry, Pixie. I shouldn't have blamed you— it was my own fault. I'll be careful from now on. I'll never let you get so hot again." She rested her cheek against Pixie's neck and stroked the soft hair on Pixie's chest.

She led Pixie back to her stall and threw her a couple of flakes of hay. Then she went outside, found a spot under a shade tree at the back of the barn, and sat down to wait for Max and Keith.

From there, she had a good view of the whole place. Megan could see someone having a lesson in the big outdoor ring. She realized that it was Amanda Sloane. Megan watched with interest. Some of the newly painted jumps had been brought into the ring. It looked as if Amanda's pony jumped whatever she pointed him at while Amanda just posed.

At last, Max and Keith appeared on the ridge beyond the barn. Why hadn't they come back to the barn sooner? Hadn't they been worried about her? Megan watched them come slowly down the hill. They didn't seem to be in any hurry at all. In fact, it looked like they were laughing!

She started to go and meet them, but then she thought better of it. She wanted Max to feel really bad for taking so long to get back and check on her. Maybe she'd even wait until tomorrow to tell him that Sharon was going to give them a lesson. She sat down to wait for him to come and find her.

But Max didn't come. At last, Megan couldn't stand it anymore. She got up and headed for the barn.

As she came in the side entrance by the wash stalls, Max and Keith were brushing off Popsicle and Penny and laughing and talking about the horse show. Megan stopped in her tracks. They weren't looking for her; they had forgotten all about her!

"Where have you guys been?" she asked, trying to keep her voice sounding neutral. She crossed her arms and waited for an answer.

"You know where we were—on a trail ride." Max began to brush Popsicle's neck.

Megan was staring at the floor; she had begun to feel as though she might cry again. "Max, why didn't you come back to the barn when Pixie ran away with me?"

"We started to, but Jake came out and told us you were okay." Max shrugged. "So we went ahead and went around the lake. There's this cool trail that goes through the pine woods. It was so much fun! Too bad you missed it."

"If you had come back for me, I could've seen it, too," Megan said sadly.

Max stopped brushing Popsicle. "If you hadn't been showing off, you would've still been with us. Meg, that was a really dumb thing you did. It's lucky that Penny and Popsicle didn't try to run away, too. Right, Keith?"

"Right," Keith agreed.

"It's not my fault Pixie's afraid of deer!" Megan exclaimed.

"It's your fault you were jumping," Max reminded her. "I told you not to. If you had listened to me, you wouldn't have scared the deer out of its hiding place."

Megan didn't know what to say. She knew Max was right.

Max turned back to his new friend. "Hey, Keith, after we get done with Penny and Popsicle, will you show me where Cuckabur is? I've been dying to see him. He's one of my favorite horses."

"Sure! I like him, too," Keith said, nodding. "He's so big! He's eighteen hands."

Megan turned and walked away from the two boys, her eyes blurry with tears. She stumbled out into the courtyard and sat down on one of the picnic tables. She couldn't ever remember feeling so lonely and left out. Her pony had run away with her, right in front of the most important person at the whole barn. She had met only one girl her age—that Amanda. Megan tried to imagine having a sleepover with Amanda, and simply couldn't. And now, even her own twin wasn't paying any attention to her.

Suddenly, she missed her old barn and her old friends worse than anything. She tried to imagine what she'd be doing right now if she were back home in Connecticut. Megan wished she could start over at Thistle Ridge Farm. But since that couldn't be, she wished she could be someplace where she felt familiar—someplace where she wouldn't keep making mistakes. "I wish I'd never seen this place," she said aloud. She laid her head on her arms and let herself cry.

7

"WHAT'S THE MATTER?" A SOFT, KIND VOICE ASKED.

Megan slowly raised her head and looked around to see who had spoken. She hadn't realized anyone else was in the courtyard. Then she saw a girl standing at the end of the picnic table. She wore a pair of very dirty beige jodhpurs a size too small for her, and a pair of scuffed and battered paddock boots that looked a couple of sizes too large. Her pale blond hair was gathered into a messy ponytail, with a few stray wisps sticking to her sweaty face. Her cheeks were flushed, as though she'd just been doing something very strenuous. The last thing Megan noticed about the girl was her eyes, which were the brightest green Megan had ever seen.

"Are you okay?" The girl spoke again. Her soft voice and her green eyes were full of concern.

Megan nodded as another tear slid down her

cheek and splashed onto her arm. She picked up her shirttail and wiped at her eyes.

"Do you want to talk about it?" the girl asked her.

"I'm just having the worst day," Megan told her.

"What happened?" The girl climbed up onto the picnic table and sat next to Megan. She was holding a soda she'd just bought from the machine under the awning by the door. Megan realized she must have walked right past her when she came outside. The girl took a big slurp of soda, then held out the can to Megan. "Want some? It's good and cold," she offered.

Megan took a swig, then handed it back. "Thanks," she said.

"I've never seen you before. I'm Chloe. What's your name?"

"Megan."

"Did you fall off? I've fallen off plenty of times. Once you get used to it, it's not so bad." Chloe grinned.

Megan shook her head. "If I had fallen off, that would've been the best thing that happened to me today," she said gloomily. "There was a whole lot of bad stuff, but the worst was my pony bolted, and I almost didn't get her stopped before she ran into the barn, and it all happened right in front of Sharon Wyndham!"

"You have a pony? Really? All your own?" Chloe asked excitedly.

"Sure. Don't you?" Megan said.

Chloe's face fell. "No, I would give *anything* to

68

have a pony of my own. But now that I'm old enough to baby-sit, I'm saving up every dollar I earn. One of these days, I hope I'll have enough to buy a pony."

"Ponies can cost hundreds or even thousands of dollars," Megan said. "It's going to take an awful lot of baby-sitting to save up that much, isn't it?"

"I already have a hundred and thirty-eight dollars saved up," Chloe said proudly.

"From baby-sitting?"

"Well, a hundred of it was a birthday present from my father. I just turned twelve in March. But I'll get there." Chloe sounded determined. "My mother always says, 'Chloe, if you want something, don't sit and complain about it—get up and do it!' So I'm going to baby-sit whenever I can." She hesitated. "Only, I'm afraid by the time I have enough money saved up, I'll be too old to ride ponies anymore," she said sadly.

"Won't your parents buy you a pony?" Megan asked. "Maybe you could pay them back."

"My parents are divorced," Chloe replied. "My little brother and I live with my mom. She can't really afford to buy me a pony. But I get to take riding lessons once a week."

"What about your dad? You said he gave you a hundred dollars." For some reason she just couldn't explain, Megan really wanted Chloe to have a pony.

Chloe was silent for a moment. Then she said, "I don't see my dad very often. He lives over in Arkansas. I guess sometimes he doesn't have a job. That

69

one time when he gave me that hundred dollars . . . Can you keep a secret?"

"Yes." Megan nodded.

Chloe lowered her voice, as if someone might be listening. "He told me he won it gambling at a casino. But he made me promise not to tell anyone, especially my mother. I don't think she'd let me keep it if she knew where it came from." Suddenly, Chloe looked anxious. "You won't tell anyone, will you, Megan?"

"I won't tell. I promise," Megan told her.

Chloe looked relieved. "Good. Because part of the money is going to be my entry fee for the horse show. You know about the horse show?"

Megan nodded. "Yes. I heard about it."

"I guess you and your pony are going to be in it," Chloe said.

"I guess so." Megan shrugged. "That's another thing. I usually do the Pony Jumpers in horse shows, and they don't even have that division here. I'll have to do the hunters, I guess, or equitation."

"I'm showing in Short Stirrup Equitation," Chloe said proudly. "I just started jumping this spring."

"What horse are you riding in the show?" Megan asked.

Chloe made a face. "I have to ride one of the school horses. And I'm supposed to pull her mane today, and I've never done it."

"I can help you," Megan said.

"Really?" Chloe smiled.

"Sure. I've pulled a lot of manes," Megan told

her. "When you get good at it, people will sometimes pay you money to do it. It's not that hard.
Braiding horses' manes for shows is a good way to
earn money, too. But braiding's a lot harder. And
you have to be *really* good at it."

"Could you teach me to braid?" Chloe asked
eagerly.

"Sure, I can teach you. It'll be good for me to
practice, too." Megan stood up and hopped off the
picnic bench. "Come on, show me where the horse
is, and we'll get to work on that mane."

Chloe got up and led Megan to a stall at the far
end of the main aisle of the barn. In the stall was
a dark bay pony with the fattest neck Megan had
ever seen. And on top of that fat neck was the
thickest, wildest mass of mane imaginable.

"This is Bo Peep," Chloe said. "She's an Ex-
moor pony."

"Oh, my," Megan said. "That is some mane.
That's going to be quite a job."

"I know," Chloe said.

Megan went and got her pulling comb, and she
and Chloe fell to work pulling the mane short and
thin so that it could be braided for the horse show.
Megan showed Chloe how to take a section of
mane, tease back the shorter hairs, and wrap the
longer ends around the comb.

"Then you just pull it out, like this." Megan
yanked out a hunk of the thick mane.

"Ouch!" Chloe watched with horror. "Doesn't it
hurt her?"

71

Megan pointed to the pony's placid expression. "If it hurt her, don't you think she'd show it? She's practically asleep." Megan pulled out another piece of mane. The pony didn't even seem to notice. "See?"

"I don't see why you can't just cut it," Chloe observed. "It would be a whole lot easier."

Megan shook her head. "You can't. It ends up looking all uneven and chopped off, no matter how straight you think you're doing it. I know, because I did it once when I was younger, to a school horse I used to ride at my old barn. Boy, did I get in trouble!" Megan giggled. "The barn manager came after *me* with the scissors. She was so mad, she almost cut off *my* hair!"

Chloe and Megan both laughed. Megan was starting to feel much happier. She liked Chloe very much. An hour later, when they finally finished pulling Bo Peep's mane, Megan knew she and Chloe were going to be great friends.

The two girls stood back and surveyed their work. "It sure does look better," Chloe said.

"Except for this middle part, where it's so thick, but I think we've done about all we can do for her," Megan said, eyeing the pony's mane critically. Bo Peep seemed to be looking back at Megan with the same expression. "She looks like she's annoyed with us for keeping her out here." Megan laughed. "Look at her."

"Sometimes I could just swear horses can understand what we're saying," Chloe said.

"I know what you mean," Megan agreed. "You know how they can look at you? And you think if they could talk, you'd know exactly what they were about to say."

"I talk to Bo Peep all the time," Chloe said. "And I just know she can understand me. Do you think that's strange?"

"No, I don't think it's strange. I talk to Pixie," Megan reassured her new friend. "And my brother, Max, talks to his horse. There are times when I'd much rather talk to horses than to people!"

"Horses always listen to you," Chloe said.

"Always," Megan agreed.

"And they're so nice to love and hug on, when you're feeling sad," Chloe added.

"Yep." Megan nodded.

"Except, I have to stay away from Bo Peep's rump, because she kicks," Chloe said. "But I don't think she really means it," she added hastily.

"Oh, well, of course, all horses kick sometimes," Megan said.

"Does your pony buck?" Chloe asked Megan.

"Not usually, except when she's turned out in the pasture. Why?" Megan asked.

"Peeps bucks," Chloe said seriously.

"Oh." Megan waited for Chloe to continue.

"She bucked me off," Chloe said. "Today, in my lesson."

"Oh. That's too bad," Megan said sympathetically. "Were you hurt?"

"No. It wasn't a very big buck, I guess." Chloe sounded unsure. "But it was kind of scary."

"Yeah, bucking is scary," Megan said, remembering how surprised she was when Pixie once bucked her off. "But if you learn to lean way back when you feel one coming, you can usually stay on."

Chloe was leaning against Bo Peep's sleek shoulder with one arm over her withers, patting the other shoulder. "I need to learn that, don't I, Peeps?" she said softly.

Megan sensed that something was bothering Chloe. "Does she do it all the time?"

Chloe shook her head. "I almost wish she did. Then at least I'd be expecting it. Megan?"

"Yes."

"What if she bucks in the horse show? What if she bucks and I fall off right in front of the judge and everybody?" Chloe sounded terrified. Megan guessed she'd been thinking about it for a long time.

"Well, what if she does buck? It's not your fault, is it? I mean, you don't smack her too hard with your crop or something, do you?" Megan asked.

"Oh, no! I mean, sometimes you have to give her a little tap to get her going, but I don't do it too hard. I just never know when it's going to happen," Chloe explained.

"Well, then, don't think about it too much. But if she does buck, lean way back, like this." Megan demonstrated with her upper body. "My trainer taught me that a horse must put its head down and stop going forward in order to buck. So if you lean way back, pick her head up, and use lots of leg to get her going again, there's no way she's going to buck you off," Megan said encouragingly. "Right?"

"Right," Chloe said doubtfully. "I guess."

"Why don't you practice what to do in your lessons?" Megan said encouragingly.

"I take group lessons, so I have to do whatever the class is working on. Besides, I don't want everyone to know I'm scared of Peeps bucking me off," Chloe said anxiously.

"Chloe, I have an idea," Megan said slowly.

"What?" Chloe looked curious.

"I think I know a way you could practice in case Bo Peep bucks with you," Megan said.

"How?" Chloe asked.

"Leave it to me," Megan said firmly. "Will you be here tomorrow?"

Chloe nodded. "I think so. Now that school is out, I can come more often. Michael, my little brother, and I stay at my grandmother's house when my mom is working, but Mamaw will let me come. I'll tell her I have to do some more stuff to get ready for the horse show."

"Good," Megan said with a satisfied expression. "Then tomorrow, when I see you, I'll help you learn to sit a buck."

"Really?" Chloe looked relieved.

"Really. I promise," Megan said.

"Good." Chloe grinned.

Just then, Amanda Sloane came into the barn

leading her fancy pony. She had forgotten to limp. She stopped and looked around for a moment.

"Hey, Amanda," Chloe said cheerfully. "I'll take him for you." Chloe hurried over to Amanda.

"Oh. There you are. Here." Amanda handed her the reins without so much as a look or a "thank you."

"Hi, Amanda," Megan said tentatively as Amanda marched past her on her way to the soda machine.

Amanda paused near Bo Peep and looked over her shoulder. "Hey," she said, as if she were doing Megan a great favor by speaking to her.

Bo Peep, who had been dozing on the cross-ties, suddenly opened her eyes. She turned her head to one side and looked around at Amanda, who was about to walk away. Then she lifted her right hind leg and kicked out in Amanda's direction, missing her by about an inch. Amanda didn't notice and just kept on walking. Bo Peep gave a satisfied snort, shook her head, and closed her eyes again.

Megan and Chloe looked at Bo Peep, then at Amanda vanishing around the corner, then at each other. Then they burst out laughing. Megan had to sit down, she was laughing so hard. When they had calmed down, Chloe said, "Do you know her?"

Megan nodded. She was still breathless from laughing. When she could speak, she asked Chloe, "Why are you doing all her work for her? The way she just handed you the reins, without even saying 'thank you' . . ."

Chloe took off Jump for Joy's bridle and clipped

his halter around his head. "I don't care what she says to me," Chloe said. "I love this pony. If I clean her saddle, she lets me groom him sometimes." She hooked up the cross-ties and took off Amanda's saddle, which she placed carefully on a saddle rack. Then she took a brush and went to work on the pony. Chloe followed each pass of the brush with a loving stroke of her hand. Megan watched curiously as Chloe groomed the pony until his white coat glowed. The pony seemed to love Chloe as much as she loved him.

"Does she ever let you ride him?" Megan asked.

"Oh, I'm not good enough to *ride* him," Chloe protested. "I'm just lucky that she lets me groom him. But one day, when I'm a more advanced rider, I hope she'll let me take care of him for her when she goes on vacation."

"Hmmm," was all Megan could think to say. She couldn't imagine cleaning tack for someone like Amanda just so she could groom her pony, no matter how wonderful he might be. Megan thought that if anyone deserved to have a horse, Chloe did. She made up her mind right then to do whatever she could to help Chloe find some way to get a pony of her own.

8

THE NEXT DAY, MEGAN WAS WAITING AT THE FRONT entrance of the barn when Chloe's grandmother drove up. Megan took Chloe's hand and dragged her through the barn, out the back door, and down the hill to the first paddock. No horses were turned out.

"Megan, what is that?" Chloe pointed to a long oak board about a foot wide that had been placed across the middle rail of the paddock fence.

Megan grinned. "That's your 'horse.' You're going to get to practice sitting through a buck. Go mount up!"

Chloe looked doubtfully at her "horse." Megan had taken Pixie's fleece cooler and borrowed two more from Max and Keith. She had wrapped them around one end of the board to widen it until it was nearly the size of a horse's barrel. Then she had piled on a couple of thick saddle pads and placed her own saddle on top of the whole pile. The girth had been a little loose, so she had taken a lead line and tied it around the saddle and the "horse" to secure it.

Megan went to one end of the board, while Chloe climbed the fence and went to the saddled end. "Are you sure this is a good idea?" she said.

"Sure I'm sure! You get on, and I'll make my end go down quickly. It'll be almost like you were sitting on a bucking horse. The 'head' will go down in front of you, the back of the 'horse' will come up behind you, and you can practice staying balanced. If we do it several times, I bet you'll get really good at it!"

"Okay . . ." Chloe mounted up tentatively.

"Ready?" Megan called out.

"I don't know," Chloe said. "I guess so."

"Just try and stay centered. You know—your ear, shoulder, hip, and heel in a vertical line." Megan quoted every riding instructor she'd ever heard. "Okay, here it comes. Stay vertical!" Megan warned. She sat down hard, and her end hit the ground. Chloe's end of the board went up suddenly. Chloe grabbed the board in front of her but was pitched forward. Her feet flew up behind her, and she rolled off and landed in the dirt. Megan jumped up and climbed over the fence. "Are you okay?" she asked anxiously.

Chloe made a face. Then she began to giggle. "That was *exactly* what happened in my lesson with

Peeps yesterday. I did the exact same thing. Boy, I bet that looked silly!"

The sound of laughter came from behind a clump of honeysuckle at the end of the paddock fence. Someone was obviously spying on them.

"Come on," Megan said, holding out her hand to help Chloe get up. Megan marched over to the clump of honeysuckle and stood with her hands on her hips. Chloe waited beside her "horse." "I know you're back there," Megan said. "You may as well come out."

Max and Keith stepped out from behind the bushes. They were still laughing. "Megan, what in the world are you trying to do?" Max said.

"I'm teaching Chloe to sit a buck. But we don't need anyone laughing at us. So you can stay and help, or you can just mind your own business," Megan told him sternly.

"Okay, okay," Max said. "We'll help. But you have to admit, it was pretty funny."

"Ready to try another one, Chloe?" Megan asked.

"I don't think so," Chloe said. "They're going to laugh at me."

"No, they won't. Will you?" Megan glared at her brother and Keith. She turned back to Chloe. "Okay. Now, remember, when the back of your 'horse' goes up, the front goes *down*. So you've got to lean back to stay vertical. Don't try to use your hands for balance. If you do, you'll be leaning forward again. Here goes."

Megan pushed her end of the board down fast.

Chloe's end went up. Chloe tipped forward a little bit but then caught herself and leaned way back. Megan gave her a few more "bucks," and each time she looked more sure of herself. Max and Keith perched on the fence and watched with interest.

"I think I'm getting it!" Chloe said enthusiastically. "Give me another one, Megan."

Megan was getting tired. "Hey, Max, Keith, come here and help me," she said to the boys.

They jumped down from the fence and went to Megan's side. "Okay, when I count to three, you help me push down this end of the board really fast."

"Got it," Max said.

"One, two . . . THREE!" Megan sat down on her end of the board. The boys pushed down at the same time. Somehow, the board slipped against the fence, sending Chloe's end flying up and sideways at the same time. Chloe locked her legs around the saddle to try and stay on, but the saddle slid around to the underside of the "horse." Chloe hung upside down by her legs for a few seconds before she plopped to the ground, flat on her back.

"Oof!" Chloe let out a gasp.

"Chloe! Are you okay?" Megan jumped up and scrambled over the fence. She knelt down beside Chloe, who squirmed on her side, trying to catch her breath. Her face looked pale, and her wide green eyes were frightened. Max and Keith lay on the ground, laughing.

Megan felt growing alarm. "Chloe, what's the matter? Can you talk?"

Chloe clutched at her stomach and coughed. Megan wondered if she should run for help. "Max, come quick! Something's wrong!"

Max quit laughing. He got up and came over to where Chloe lay on the ground. "She couldn't be hurt," he said uneasily. "She only fell a few feet."

Keith joined them. Chloe was now groaning a little, but the color was coming back into her face. "I think she just got the wind knocked out of her," he offered.

Megan helped Chloe into a sitting position. "Feel better?"

"Yeah. Boy, that was scary. For a minute there, I couldn't get any air."

"You sure scared *me*," Megan told her.

"I'm glad Peeps doesn't buck like *that*," Chloe said. "I think I could stay on her no matter what she does after that!"

They untacked the "horse" and put away the board. Everybody was thirsty, so they got sodas and went to sit in the barn where it was cooler.

Keith and Chloe started talking about the horse show. Megan and Max told how they had ridden in their first horse show when they were just five years old. "We went in the lead-line class, where a handler goes along beside you," Max explained. "I got a blue ribbon."

"I got a pink!" Megan said. "It was my favorite color, so I was happy!"

"That's fifth place," Keith observed.

"Who cares?" Megan said. "I never think about the ribbons when I'm in the show ring. I'm just having fun!"

"This will be my first horse show," Chloe said. "And I've had butterflies in my stomach for about a week now! Actually, the more I think about the show, the more they start to feel like bats!"

"Don't worry, Chloe. Everyone gets nervous about showing," Megan reassured her. "You're showing in the Short Stirrup classes, right?"

Chloe nodded.

"Well so am I," Megan told her, "so I'll be right there with you."

"So will I," Keith offered.

"We'll all help you Chloe," Max said. "We have lots of experience showing in Short Stirrup."

"We'll be the Short Stirrup Club," Megan said. "And we'll all look out for each other. So don't worry about it anymore, Chloe."

"Yeah, you're going to be fine. You'll ride circles around Amanda Sloane," Keith said.

"What do you mean?" Chloe asked.

"Amanda Sloane's showing in Short Stirrup, too, and you're going to beat her, right guys?" Keith looked around for approval.

"Right," Megan said firmly. "With a little help from the Short Stirrup Club," she added.

"I'm not going to beat Amanda Sloane! She's

much better than I am. I haven't got a chance against her," Chloe protested.

"She's not that good," Megan said. "I was watching her ride yesterday. She just poses. Her pony's perfect, but if he ever did do anything wrong, I bet she'd just fall apart."

"That pony is so good, and so pretty," Chloe said longingly. "And she is so mean to him. She just yanks him around all the time. And she never even grooms him or anything. I don't know why somebody so mean deserves to have such a nice pony."

"She doesn't deserve it," Keith said. "She's just lucky enough to have rich parents. They buy her everything."

"If I had a pony, I would never treat it like that," Chloe said indignantly. "I would love it and take care of it. Even if it was ugly and it bucked," she added.

"You know, she just needs one more blue ribbon in the Pony Hunters to win the Champion of the Year award. And you know she's going to get it. And then she'll be impossible to be around," Keith said.

"She's already impossible to be around," Megan muttered.

"Who's impossible?" a voice said. They all looked up. There stood Amanda Sloane, in a pair of perfectly clean, very expensive pale gray jodhpurs and a pastel purple riding shirt with a monogrammed collar. Her blond hair was pulled back in two perfect French braids, with matching purple ribbons at the ends. Her paddock boots looked as if she had just had them polished.

"Oh, hey, Amanda," Keith said.

"Hey, Keith. Hey, Chloe." Amanda tilted her head to the side and smiled a fake-friendly smile.

Max noticed that she wore braces, the expensive kind that are nearly invisible, though he couldn't see why she needed them. Her teeth looked perfectly straight, as far as he could tell.

Suddenly, he realized Amanda was looking at him. She was still smiling that sickly sweet smile. "I don't believe I've met you," she said, stepping closer to him. "I am Amanda Susannah Sloane. You can call me Mandy, though."

"I'm Max," Max said, uneasily backing away from her. "Why, what a coincidence!" Amanda followed him. "We have a German shepherd named Max. Now isn't that funny?"

Megan made a curious snorting sound and covered her mouth, pretending to sneeze. She was trying not to laugh out loud. "Bless you," Chloe said helpfully. Max glared at his sister.

"Is this your horse?" Amanda peered over the top board to look at Popsicle.

"Yes," Max said proudly. "This is Popsicle."

"Popsicle? What a precious name! Now, what divisions do you show in?"

"Children's Hunters," Max said. "And the Children's Equitation."

"Well, now! I'll be seeing you in the Children's

Hunters, won't I? I'll be showing my pony, Jump for Joy. You've heard of him, haven't you?"

"No."

"Well, I guess you will soon."

"Actually, I'll be judged against the horses." Max seemed relieved. "If you have a pony, I won't be riding against you."

"Well, then, I could cheer you on," Amanda said.

"I'll be in the pony division with you, Amanda. So will Chloe," Megan said.

"Yes, I know." Amanda turned to look at Megan. "I've heard about your pony. I heard she's dangerous. Do you think you'll be able to control her in the show ring? My mother is concerned that you may be unsafe."

"Of course I can control her!" Megan snapped.

"Pixie spooked at a deer," Chloe added. "Just because she's not used to seeing them is no reason to say she's dangerous. She can't help it. She just has to get used to them."

"I didn't know you were such an expert," Amanda said to Chloe. "Don't you ride in that group class, the one Leigh teaches? You know Leigh used to be a *groom*, don't you? Did you know that? Your riding instructor is really a groom. Of course, my mother says it was considerate of Sharon to give her a chance. It's too bad you couldn't take lessons from Sharon. But then, my mother says you have to *pay* for *quality*."

"Mandeeee? Amandaaa! Where are you?" It was Mrs. Sloane.

"I have to go now, Max. It's time for my private lesson with Sharon Wyndham," Amanda said, ignoring everyone else. "It was nice to meet you. Maybe we can go on a trail ride together, and then you can come over for dinner. All right?"

"Huh?" Max said.

"Good," Amanda said. "I'll call you tonight, and we can plan it. 'Bye," she called, and strutted down the aisle.

"Hey, Max, is that your new girlfriend?" Keith teased.

"No way!" Max said, sounding alarmed. "I never even saw her before."

"I can't believe anybody could be so mean!" Megan was fuming. "I hope she doesn't win a thing at the horse show. She doesn't deserve it! I hope you beat her, Chloe! Wouldn't that show her?"

"I could never beat her," Chloe said sadly. "She rides all the time. She trains with Sharon Wyndham. She has that beautiful pony. How could somebody like me compete with that? She even has perfect clothes. Look at me. These are the only riding clothes I have, and the boots are too big, and the pants are too small. I'll look ridiculous in them. I don't even know why I'm doing this stupid horse show!" She jumped off the tack trunk and ran out the side door by the wash stalls.

"Poor Chloe," Keith said.

"We have to do something," Megan said emphatically.

"Like what?" Max asked.

"She has to ride in the horse show," Megan said. "She's been working so hard to get ready for it. And we spent all that time teaching her what to do in case Bo Peep bucks."

"She's a good rider," Keith said. "I've seen her in her lessons."

"She just doesn't feel confident, especially after Amanda said all those mean things," Max said.

"Right," Megan said. "We have to help her feel confident. Here's what I think we should do . . ."

Max and Keith bent their heads close to Megan while she explained her idea in a low voice. Then the two boys went in one direction, while Megan went to look for Chloe. She found her in Bo Peep's stall, weeping against the animal's broad neck.

"Chloe?" She came slowly into the stall, remembering to stay far away from Bo Peep's hindquarters. Chloe answered with a little sob. Megan put a hand on her shoulder. "Chloe, I know you must feel terrible. That was the meanest thing I ever heard anybody say. It's not your fault you don't have fancy clothes or the best trainer."

"I love Leigh!" Chloe said furiously. "She's a great trainer! I don't care if she used to be a groom. She probably knows more about horses than somebody who's only been an instructor and never did any other jobs around horses."

"She probably does," Megan agreed. "And you know what? Sharon Wyndham used to be a groom, too."

Chloe was silent for a moment. "How can that be?" she asked.

"It's true," Megan said. "And everybody knows about it. I read it in *Horse and Pony* magazine. There was a big article on her, and it told all about her background. She spent a whole year in Pennsylvania as a working student for a famous trainer. She had to do everything, including mucking stalls and scrubbing water buckets. In return, she got to ride his horses and take lessons from him. That's how she got started doing the big jumper shows."

Chloe peeked out from under Bo Peep's mane. "Really?" she said doubtfully.

"Really," Megan said. "So you shouldn't even think twice about what that Amanda said."

"Well, I know Leigh is a good instructor. But Amanda has the best of everything. I don't want to compete with that." Chloe looked like she was going to cry again.

"Chloe, somebody can have all the best stuff, but it doesn't make them the best rider," Megan said emphatically. "My instructor always said, 'You don't go in a horse show to win. You go in a horse show to do your best and have fun. You win if you learn something.'"

"I want to be in the horse show," Chloe said. She gave a couple of little hiccuping breaths. She had been crying hard. "I just don't want to look silly."

Megan put her arm around her friend's shoulders. "You won't, Chloe, I promise."

"How do you know?" Chloe asked.

"You promise not to back out of doing the show?" Megan said sternly.

Chloe wiped her eyes, and nodded.

Megan grinned. "Then leave everything to me."

9

THE REST OF THE WEEK WENT BY QUICKLY. MEGAN AND Max took a lesson with Sharon Wyndham. She was a wonderful trainer, just as they had imagined she would be. But she was very strict. Megan could tell she was the sort of trainer who wouldn't put up with *any* nonsense. She said something to Max once during the lesson, when Sharon was setting up a fence. Sharon turned around and said quietly, "There is no talking during your lesson, unless I ask you a direct question. That way, you will be sure to hear everything I have to say to you. All right?"

Megan nodded. She made up her mind not to say another word unless Sharon asked her a question. She sat quietly on Pixie as Sharon spoke to her brother.

"Now, Max. Pick up a left lead canter and go up

over the outside line." Sharon pointed to the jumps as she described the course. "Then down over the brush box on the diagonal, then up over the other outside line, and back down this first line coming toward the in-gate. Got it?"

He nodded. Megan thought that finally Max looked happy. Popsicle's knee was almost healed, and they were doing what they loved best—jumping around a hunter course. She watched with envy as Max and Popsicle sailed around the little course. Max loved doing things right, and it showed. Popsicle gave him a perfect flying change of lead as he changed direction after the diagonal fence. They jumped down the last line, made a smooth transition to rising trot, circled once, then walked.

"That's a good little hunter you have there, Max. You should do well on Saturday." Sharon nodded her approval as Max let Popsicle stretch the reins all the way through his fingers and gave him a big, satisfied pat on the neck.

"All right, Miss Megan, your turn." Sharon nodded at her.

Megan took a deep breath and gathered up the reins. Sharon had put a different bit on Pixie, and the pony tossed her head impatiently as she felt the curb chain under her chin. She was still fussing with the bit and tossing her head as Megan trotted a circle, then picked up a canter. She glanced over at Chloe, who was sitting on the fence with Keith, watching the lesson. Chloe smiled at her and gave her a discreet thumbs-up signal.

She headed for the first fence, wishing she could jump around as smoothly as Max had just done. Max and Popsicle had made it look like a dream. Megan's round felt more to her like a hunter course nightmare!

Pixie had her head as high up as the martingale would allow. She put four and even three strides in the lines that Max had done in fives and sixes. She couldn't seem to settle down no matter how much Megan "talked" to her with her hands. She got the lead change after the diagonal fence, then changed back to the wrong lead at the rail. Then she almost ran out on the last line because she was off balance. Through it all, Megan felt her hands getting jerked by Pixie tossing her head.

At the very last fence, she jumped from so far away that Megan got "left behind" and had to let the reins slip through her fingers to keep from yanking Pixie's mouth. She came down hard and lost a stirrup, then she couldn't get Pixie back down to a trot because her reins were so long. *What a disaster!* she thought to herself as she pulled up in the middle of the ring. Megan patted Pixie dejectedly and waited to hear what Sharon would say.

Sharon gave Megan the one high eyebrow. Then she spoke. "Well. That could've been a little slower," she said. "This pony is one of the best jumpers I've seen in a while. But you can't just let her find her own way around a jump course. Your upper body is very forward." Sharon demonstrated from the ground. "You need to sit up and ride

93

through the turns with your leg instead of steering her around with the reins."

Megan watched Sharon carefully and corrected her position. Sharon nodded approvingly at Megan's position and continued, "You can help your pony feel calmer about her job if you work on just taking your time getting around the course. It'll improve your performance in the jumper classes, too. The secret to jumpers is not speed. It's balance and rhythm. A horse that's balanced can lengthen or shorten its stride, or turn on a dime, without seeming to hurry at all."

"That makes a lot of sense," Megan agreed.

"Good." Sharon nodded briskly. "Now, let's work on it. Let me see you jump this course again, but this time, make every stride come from you. You're not a passenger up there, you're the driver."

"Okay," Megan said. She really thought she understood what Sharon meant. She picked up a canter and started the course again, but this time, she chose a very quiet canter and concentrated on making Pixie stay in that rhythm. By about the third fence, Pixie had stopped tossing her head. Megan took a deep breath and told herself to relax. At the same moment, she felt the reins get lighter as Pixie settled into a quiet working canter.

Megan knew her pony well, but at that moment, she felt connected with her in a way she'd never felt before. She was no longer a person riding a horse; she *was* the horse. Pixie was moving to the left or right at the smallest signal from Megan's leg. Megan could feel Pixie's hindquarters swinging rhythmically under her seat at every stride, and she knew exactly when each jump was going to happen. Megan finished the course and made the transition to posting trot and then to the walk. She was grinning hugely as she let the reins out and gave Pixie a great big hug. Pixie dropped her head and snorted several times, as if she felt the same way.

From the fence, Keith and Chloe applauded. Max held out a hand for a high-five as she parked Pixie next to him again. She knew she'd done it.

"Megan Morrison," said Sharon, "that was *so much better*. Did you feel it?"

Megan nodded, still grinning, and gave Pixie another huge pat.

"And Megan," Sharon added, "when you show me you can ride through hunter and equitation courses like that every time, I'll start adding a Pony Jumper division to my shows." She winked at Megan.

The rest of the week, the barn absolutely hummed with activity. Grooms stood on stepladders and upside-down buckets, busy clipping the fuzz from horses' ears and the long whiskers from their muzzles. On Friday, big horse transport vans started to arrive, with the horses and ponies from other stables too far away to make the drive on Saturday morning.

When they arrived at the barn, Max and Megan joined Chloe and Keith over by the schooling ring.

The ring was full of trainers and riders schooling horses and ponies. The four friends sat on the top rail of the fence and watched.

"I've never seen so many horses going in so many directions at once," Chloe said in amazement. "I don't know how they keep from crashing into each other."

"It looks crazy, but there is a kind of system of rules, so that doesn't happen," Max told her. "For instance, you always pass left shoulder to left shoulder."

"And when you're jumping, you yell out which fence you're taking so everybody knows to stay out of the way," Megan added.

"Boy, you two sure know a lot about horse shows," Chloe said appreciatively.

Megan and Max shrugged their shoulders. At that moment, they looked very much alike.

"We've been to so many,'" Megan said.

"After a while, you just pick it up," Max agreed.

"Will y'all help me tomorrow if I don't know what to do?" Chloe asked. She sounded anxious.

"Of course we will," Megan reassured her. "Won't we, guys?"

"Yep," Keith said. He caught Max's eye and winked at him. Megan tried not to smile.

Chloe frowned. "What are y'all looking at me like that for? You look like the cat that ate the canary."

"Never mind," Megan said quickly. "It's getting late, and I promised to help you braid Bo Peep's mane. Let's get started, because I still have to braid Pixie."

Max went with Keith to bathe Penny, while Megan found a skein of black yarn and showed Chloe how to braid. Chloe's first braid was too loose, so she had to pull it out and start over. The next one slipped before she could get it tied. By the third try, she made a neat braid and managed to get it tied off. "There. How's that, Megan?"

"That's a good one," Megan told her. "Just don't make them any bigger than that. Fat braids don't look as nice as tiny ones. You keep working on her. I'm going to get started on Pixie."

Megan went to work on her own pony's mane. Keith came by leading Penny, who was shiny-clean from her bath. "Did you get it?" she asked him.

"Yeah," Keith said. "At first, Haley couldn't find it, but then she did. I brought it—it's in a bag in my trunk."

"Good!" Megan said. After a while, she went to check on Chloe. Megan showed Chloe how to pull the ends of the yarn through the top of the braid and tie it off to form a little bump at the top.

"Oh, that looks so pretty!" Chloe exclaimed.

"It does," Megan agreed. "I love how they look when they're braided."

"Even Bo Peep looks elegant," Chloe said.

Max was braiding Popsicle when Megan returned. "I don't know who thought of this," he grumbled, "but I wish they never had. I hate braiding. It looks so dorky."

"You always say that," Megan observed. "But then when you're finished, you always say, 'Doesn't he look great?'"

"I know." Max sighed. "I just hate braiding. My fingers get so tired."

"Poor little thing," Megan teased him. She climbed up on the upside-down bucket she'd been using to reach the mane behind Pixie's ears and went to work on the last few braids.

"Maybe I'll just leave him unbraided," Max decided. "Lots of people don't braid for shows now, anyway."

"Not people who ride for Thistle Ridge Farm."

Max blushed as he turned to see Sharon Wyndham standing in the aisle, holding a diet soda she had just bought from the machine. She had been working all day getting things ready for the show. Megan had seen her moving jumps around, directing the people from other barns where to park and unload, riding at least two different horses, and once mucking out a stall. Megan wondered how in the world Sharon could be that busy all day and still manage to keep her clothes clean and be wearing fresh lipstick. She didn't even have helmet hair; her blond ponytail looked as neat as ever.

Megan's own clothes were filthy. A wavy lock of hair that had slipped out of her ponytail refused to stay behind her ear, no matter how many times she tucked it back. She wiped her sweaty face on her shirtsleeve and wished she could look like Sharon.

Sharon took a sip of the soda. "This is not just

a schooling show. This is an important show because it's the last in the winter–spring series. You will be making an impression on a lot of people tomorrow. I expect you all to look and act like professionals. And Max, you are going to braid that horse."

"Yes, ma'am," Max said.

"Then why are you standing there?" Sharon smiled. "Pitter-patter, let's get at 'er! Keith, come with me for a minute, will you, please?"

Keith and Sharon disappeared for a few minutes, then came back with an armful of cold sodas. "Here's a little inspiration for you." Sharon handed them each a soda, including Chloe, who had come to tell Megan that she was finished with Bo Peep's mane.

"She is amazing," Megan said, watching Sharon head back to the office. "One day, I'm going to have a barn like this and be just like her."

"What's it like taking lessons from her?" Chloe asked.

"Great," Megan , Max, and Keith said at the same time. Then they laughed.

"I'm finished," Megan said, jumping off the bucket.

"She looks beautiful," Chloe said, admiring Pixie's braids.

Megan stroked her mare's pretty, arched neck. She'd given Pixie a bath that morning after she rode, and her coat was soft and shiny. Megan gave

Pixie a kiss on the end of her dark velvet muzzle. "I love you," she said. "I love you, I love you!"

The girls put Pixie away and helped Max finish braiding. It took the three of them less than half an hour to finish, right down to the forelock.

"Thanks a lot," Max said gratefully. "If you two hadn't helped me, I'd have been doing this for hours." It was getting dark outside. Max yawned. "Now I'm ready to go home and go to sleep."

"I'm starving," Megan said.

"I'm too nervous to eat," Chloe said. "And I don't know how in the world I'm going to sleep. I'm too excited."

"You'd better try," Megan said.

"Yeah, you're going to show Amanda Sloane how to ride tomorrow, right?" Keith reminded her.

"Oh, no." Chloe groaned. "Please, can we talk about something else? If I think about her or this show anymore, I may throw up."

"You'll do great, I promise," Megan reassured her.

"Megan, Dad's here," Max called.

"Stop worrying," Megan told Chloe, giving her a quick hug. "You're going to be great! Just wait and see."

10

MAX WAS UP AND DRESSED IN HIS SHOW CLOTHES BY SIX o'clock in the morning. He woke up his sister, put on coffee for his parents, and was on his second bowl of cereal by the time Megan came downstairs. "Garters, Meg," he reminded her without looking up.

She turned without saying a word and marched upstairs. In a minute, she was back, this time with leather garter straps buckled around her jodhpurs just below the knee. Max had been given tall boots for his last birthday, so he didn't show in jodhpurs anymore. He held out his old garter straps to Megan. "For Chloe," he explained when she gave him a puzzled look.

Megan thanked him with a smile and put them into her backpack. She yawned and poured herself a glass of juice. Although talkative at other times, she was quiet in the morning. She had once explained that her thoughts needed time to wake up before they could come out of her mouth. Max passed her the cereal box. "Did you remember the clothes?"

Megan nodded at her backpack and poured herself a bowl of cereal.

In another minute, James Morrison came downstairs. He paused in the doorway. "Do I smell coffee?" He gave his son an inquiring look.

Max pointed to the coffee maker. "I'm way ahead of you, Dad."

James Morrison went straight to the coffee maker and poured himself a cup. "I don't know how I'd survive your horse shows if you weren't so organized, Max," he said, sitting down with his children. He gestured toward Megan. "She talking yet?"

"Not yet," Max said. "We're lucky."

James Morrison was looking with admiration at his son's attire. Max wore his boots and breeches, a navy blue show jacket, and a crisp white shirt with a navy and burgundy tie. "Max, sometime you must show me how you knot your tie," he said. "Mine never come out looking quite so neat."

"Sure thing, Dad. Are you dropping us at the barn?" Max asked.

"Yes. I've been nominated by your other parental unit, who spent the night operating on someone's hip bone. She'll meet us there later."

Megan finished her juice and stood up. Her

voice, when she was ready to use it, worked just fine. "Let's go, guys! It's almost seven o'clock!"

"It talks!" Max said, pretending to be horrified. "Run, Dad! Quick! The Bronco! It's our only hope!"

The three of them ran laughing to the Bronco. James Morrison dropped them off at the barn, promising to return in time for their first class. The twins hurried into the barn, which now seemed even busier than the night before.

They took Pixie and Popsicle out and began brushing them. Keith was already there, tacking up Penny. Megan asked if he had seen Chloe yet, but he said he hadn't.

Megan and Max had their horses tacked and were ready to go down to the schooling ring when Chloe came slowly down the aisle. She wore her too-small jodhpurs with a pink blouse and a rather large navy blue blazer that was not a real riding jacket. She had polished her boots as well as she could.

"Chloe! Hi!" Megan said cheerfully. "I was wondering where you were."

Chloe's face was pale, and the freckles on her nose stood out. Her green eyes were huge and frightened, and a little red, as though she had been crying. "I look terrible, don't I?" she said soberly. Her voice was barely above a whisper. "Megan, I don't think I can do this. Everybody else has all the right clothes. I don't even have a real riding jacket."

Megan handed Pixie's reins to Max and slung her backpack over one shoulder. "Come with me," she said. She grabbed Chloe by the hand and dragged her into the small bathroom between the two wash stalls, closing the door behind them.

"But I don't have to go to the bathroom," Chloe protested.

"I don't either," Megan said.

"Then what are we doing in here?" Chloe asked.

"I have something for you." Megan unzipped her backpack and pulled out a pair of beige jodhpurs with leather knee patches. She handed them to Chloe, saying, "These should fit you. They were Max's show jodhpurs from last year, but he wears boots and breeches now, and they're a little small for me. Go ahead and try them on."

Chloe unlaced her boots and pulled off her old jodhpurs. She put on the ones Megan gave her and stood up straight. "How do they look? Do they fit?"

"They look like they were made for you." Megan reached into the backpack again. "Here, try the shirt."

Megan pulled out a white show shirt with a little band collar. Chloe put it on. "Now put your boots back on," Megan ordered. When the boots were on, Megan knelt and buckled Max's garters just below Chloe's knees.

"Is it your shirt?" Chloe asked.

"It used to be." Megan smiled. "Now it's yours. I never wear it anyway." She took a little gold pin in the shape of a horseshoe from her pocket and pinned it in the center of Chloe's collar. "This always brought me luck," she said.

Chloe touched the little pin. "It's so pretty. But don't you need it?"

"I have this one that my grandmother gave me." Megan lifted her chin so that Chloe could see the pin on her own collar. "My grandmother used to ride when she was a young girl in Ireland. Her mother gave it to her at her very first horse show, and she gave it to me for my birthday this year."

"How do I look?" Chloe asked.

"Like you're almost ready for a horse show! Come with me." Megan grabbed her backpack. Chloe picked up her clothes and followed. When they reached the aisle where Keith and Max were waiting, Megan put her hands over Chloe's eyes. Keith went into his trunk and pulled out a navy blue riding jacket. Max put it on Chloe. Then Megan took her hands away from Chloe's eyes. She slowly opened them and looked down at herself. A little smile started at one corner of her mouth and spread over her whole face.

"Chloe, you look great!" Megan said.

"The jacket fits you perfectly," Keith said.

"But whose is it?" Chloe asked.

"It's Haley's old jacket." Keith shrugged. "She outgrew it a couple of years ago. It's just been hanging around. She said you could have it."

"Really? I can really have it?" Chloe's smile grew wider.

"Sure." Keith returned the smile.

"You look very professional," Max said approvingly.

"Thank y'all, so much." Chloe was beaming. "It's the nicest thing anybody ever did for me. Oh, wait until my mama sees me!"

"Oh!" Keith said. "I almost forgot." He dug into the pocket of his jacket and pulled out a pair of brown leather riding gloves. "Here," he said, handing them to Chloe.

"Oh, I couldn't take your gloves," she protested.

"Once I lost one, so I got another pair, and then I found the lost one," Keith explained. "So now I have two pairs. You may as well take these. I can only wear one pair at a time. Besides, I don't even like to wear gloves. I only use them in shows."

Chloe thanked him and put on the gloves. "Go get Bo Peep. We'll meet you down at the schooling ring," Megan said.

A few minutes later, the four of them were warming up in the busy schooling ring. It had rained hard sometime in the night, leaving puddles everywhere. Horses and ponies slogged through the slushy sand.

Sharon Wyndham stood near a jump, shouting instructions at Amanda Sloane, who was trotting around on her perfectly groomed and braided pony. She made a sharp turn at the wettest end of the ring, and the pony stumbled, but he caught himself and went on.

"Amanda, I told you to watch the footing! You're going to lame that pony turning through the puddles like that! Please be more careful!" Sharon scolded her. "Now come down over the cross-rail," she instructed.

Amanda trotted to the end of the ring. Her expression was blank. She didn't seem to be paying any attention to Sharon. She turned the pony sharply and headed for the fence.

"Amanda!" Sharon closed her eyes for a moment as though she were in great pain. Then she opened them in time to see Amanda jump the cross-rail. "That's enough for you, I think. Walk him around for a few minutes, and then go put him away for a little while." Sharon motioned for Megan, Max, and Keith to come into the ring.

"Chloe, where's Leigh?" Sharon called to her.

"I saw her in the barn. She said she was on the way down."

"Well, come on in and start warming up. I'll keep an eye on you 'til she gets down here," Sharon offered.

Chloe came into the ring, looking pleased. Sharon took a good look at her attire and exclaimed, "Chloe Goodman, don't you look elegant on that pony!"

"Thank you," Chloe said shyly.

They all began to warm up. After they had spent a few minutes trotting and cantering in both directions, Sharon had them jump the cross-rail. Then she made it a vertical. "Okay, Megan and Max, you can take turns coming over this vertical. Chloe, why don't you hop off and put Bo Peep away. I believe you've done enough with her. And when you get up to the barn, find out what's keeping Leigh, will you? I need her to come down here."

"I will," Chloe said. "Thank you for schooling me, Miss Sharon."

"You can call me Sharon. You're welcome," she said.

Chloe dismounted by the side of the warm-up fence, where she wouldn't be in the way. She ran up Bo Peep's stirrups and loosened the girth. Then she waited for an opening so that she could cross the busy track to the gate to go out. There were so many horses going back and forth, she couldn't cross, though the gate was only fifteen feet away from her. She stood patiently.

Sharon suddenly noticed that Amanda was still in the ring. "Amanda, I thought I told you to go up to the barn." Sharon frowned. "Please listen." She turned to tell another rider something.

"Heads up, the vertical!" A rider on a big bay came cantering down toward the warm-up fence where Chloe stood. The rider seemed to be having a lot of trouble keeping the horse under control. They were coming very fast. Just then, Amanda Sloane cut across the ring toward the gate. She was about to walk right in front of the jump!

"Amanda! Watch out!" Chloe yelled.

"Heads up, HEADS UP!" the rider yelled.

Amanda didn't seem to hear either of them. In another second, she would cross right in front of the jump, just as the rider on the bay would be jumping it. The rider on the bay was wrestling with her horse, trying to pull up, but the horse looked set on the jump and actually sped up. It looked like there was about to be a terrible accident.

Suddenly, Chloe dropped Bo Peep's reins, crossed in front of the fence, and grabbed Jump for Joy's reins, pulling him to a stop. The big bay jumped the fence, landing in a puddle just a couple of feet from Chloe, and cantered away. Megan and Max hurried over to see if Chloe was all right.

"What are you doing?" Amanda said crossly to Chloe. "Let go!" She seemed completely unaware that she had almost caused a serious accident.

Chloe let go of the pony's reins and stood trembling. Sharon caught Bo Peep, who stood quietly where Chloe had left her, and hurried to Chloe's side. "Are you all right? That was very close." Sharon put a hand on her shoulder. "Chloe?"

"I think so." She seemed stunned. A big glob of mud was plastered to her cheek. She wiped it off with a shaking hand. Then she slowly looked down at herself. Her new show clothes were splattered with mud from the horse landing so close to her. "Oh," she said softly.

"Oh, Chloe," Megan said. "Your nice new show clothes."

"It's just my luck," Chloe said. She tried hard to smile, but they could all see the disappointment in her face.

"Chloe, that was really brave of you to stop Amanda's pony," Max told her.

"I'm just so glad I was able to stop him. I couldn't stand for him to get hurt." She shuddered and gave Jump for Joy a pat with the hand that wasn't muddy.

Just then, Chloe's trainer, Leigh, came running over. "Is she okay?" Leigh asked. "How did she fall off?"

"She didn't fall off," Sharon said.

When Sharon explained what Chloe had done, Leigh hugged her. "Brave girl!" she said. "Never mind about your clothes. You have a little time before your classes. Come on, let's see if we can get you cleaned up." She took Bo Peep's reins, put an arm around Chloe's shoulders, and headed for the barn. As they were leaving the ring, Megan saw the rider on the strong bay horse go over and ask if everyone was all right.

The only one who didn't seem concerned was Amanda, who had caused the whole thing in the first place. Amanda just sat there, playing with the unbraided lock of mane on Jump for Joy's withers.

"Well? What do you have to say for yourself?" Sharon demanded.

"I'm sorry," Amanda said, not sounding it in the least. "I'll never do it again." She yawned daintily.

Sharon gave an exasperated sigh. "You'd better not. Now, get out of this ring before you cause some real damage."

They all left the ring. No one had to wait to cross the track, because almost everyone in the ring was gone. The horse show was about to begin!

11

THE LOUDSPEAKER CAME ON WITH A CRACKLE AND A whine, then Jake's voice boomed out over the farm: "Good morning, ladies and gentlemen. Welcome to Thistle Ridge Farm!"

Megan and Keith found a spot where they could stand and watch the Lead-line class. Megan always loved seeing the littlest children in their tiny paddock boots and riding jackets perched on top of quiet ponies or gentle old horses. When the class was done, the judge awarded each child a blue ribbon. Megan thought that was a great idea, but one little boy began to cry. His handler asked him what was the matter, and he managed to sob, "But I wanted a green one!"

Everybody who heard him laughed. Someone found a green ribbon and gave it to the little boy, who happily traded in his blue ribbon. His handler led him out as Jake announced the Short Stirrup division, calling the riders in for their first class. Megan looked around for Chloe. Finally, she saw her coming down the hill on Bo Peep, with Leigh and Max. She waited for them to get to the ring, so she could give Chloe a thumbs-up.

Megan entered the ring and automatically looked for a space among the other riders where she wouldn't be crowded. In a moment, the ringmaster called out, "You are now being judged at the walk." Megan sat up and tried to look her best. At the trot, she glanced at Pixie's outside shoulder for a moment to be sure she had the correct diagonal, then glued her legs to Pixie's sides as she trotted by the judge. *Heels down, toes in, eyes up, hands quiet,* she thought to herself, wondering for the hundredth time how anyone could do all that and manage to stay relaxed at the same time.

Pixie was excited to be in the show ring; Megan kept passing other riders. She passed Amanda Sloane, who still had a blank look on her face. She saw Chloe and noted that she seemed to be doing just fine. There were about fourteen riders in the class, which Megan knew was pretty big. In a moment, half of the riders were asked to stand in the middle, while the other half cantered. Megan, Amanda, and Chloe were all in the first group. They cantered in one direction. Megan couldn't see Chloe, but she heard Leigh at the rail tell someone, "Use your stick!" If it was Chloe, Megan hoped Bo Peep wouldn't buck.

When the riders reversed direction, Megan was a good distance behind Chloe. She saw Amanda cantering right behind Bo Peep, until Jump for Joy's nose was almost in Bo Peep's tail. Bo Peep pinned her ears flat against her head in annoyance. She was just about ready to kick. Megan knew that a good rider would never ride so close to another horse for that very reason. Chloe gave Bo Peep a thump with her heels to try and keep her going forward. Then Amanda turned toward the inside so that she was cantering right beside Chloe, blocking the judge's view of her. She passed her and moved back to the rail right in front of Bo Peep, cutting her off. Chloe had to pull up to keep from running into her.

Megan knew that to cut off another rider in the show ring is terribly bad manners. It counts against the rider if the judge sees it, because it's dangerous and interferes with other riders. The judge had been looking down when Amanda moved in front of Bo Peep; he looked up just in time to see that Chloe was trotting when they were supposed to be cantering. He wrote something down on his card. Then Megan had to canter a circle to get a space for herself, so she couldn't see Chloe anymore until they were lined up in the middle again.

When the class was over, Megan dismounted and went to find Chloe. She was standing beside Peeps. "I saw what happened when we were cantering," Megan told her. "Amanda cut you off. There was no way you could've kept from breaking the canter.

What she did was so unfair. It's just too bad the judge didn't see it. She never should have won that class!"

Megan was furious with Amanda. Chloe surely would have won a ribbon if Amanda hadn't interfered with her round. But to Megan's surprise, Chloe looked happy. "Megan, did you see what happened in the first canter?"

Megan shook her head. "No. What happened?"

"Well, the ringmaster said to canter, and Peeps wouldn't. So I had to use my stick, and guess what happened?" Chloe's smile grew wider.

"She cantered?" Megan guessed.

"No! She bucked!" Chloe laughed. "A great big buck, right in front of the judge! And I stayed on! It was easy; it was just like you said. I stuck right on, and then she cantered!"

"Hooray for you, Chloe!" Megan congratulated her.

"Megan, I don't think I'm scared of bucking anymore," Chloe said. "I'm so glad! I can't wait for my next class."

The next two classes were jump classes. Megan was still upset. She had trouble focusing on her riding. Everything seemed to distract her. Pixie seemed to feel the same way. Neither she nor Megan performed well. In one class, Megan lost a stirrup, which she knew meant she wouldn't place. Amanda had two flawless rounds, mostly because of her pony, and ended up being Short Stirrup Champion.

"You could have beaten her easily," Max said. "What happened? I've never seen you look so nervous."

"Don't you think I know that? Just leave me alone, all right?" Megan was furious with herself. For the first time, she wasn't having fun at a horse show.

"Whatever you say." Max gave her a puzzled look and went to study the jump courses for the Children's Hunters.

Popsicle and Max ended up with two yellow third-place ribbons in the Hunters. Max was satisfied with that, since the classes were large. When the horses had finished, the jump crew came out and lowered the fences for the ponies. Megan and Chloe were mounted and ready. Amanda was also there, with Mrs. Sloane hovering over her, giving advice as she brushed off Amanda's spotless jacket.

Megan glanced at Chloe's riding clothes. She had managed to get most of the mud off her jacket, but the jodhpurs still had a big smear across one leg. Megan had been trying to calm down, but now she felt herself getting angry all over again. Chloe had risked getting hurt herself to save Amanda from being in a serious accident. And Amanda hadn't even thanked her! Chloe's new riding clothes were splattered with mud because of Amanda. And because of Amanda, Chloe had been eliminated from winning a ribbon in her first class.

"It's not fair," Megan murmured through clenched teeth. Chloe worked so hard and had so little. Amanda won championships because all she had to do was pose and let her perfect pony carry her around. Now Amanda only needed one more blue ribbon, and she would win Pony Hunter Champion of the Year.

Megan felt her heart thumping with anger. She had never thought twice about how she placed in a horse show. She had always just been happy to be riding. But suddenly, for the first time, she wanted to *win*. Even more, she wanted to beat Amanda.

Max came over and stood by Megan near the in-gate. "Mom and Dad are here," he said. "Did you see them?"

Megan wouldn't take her eyes off the course. Amanda was about to enter the ring. "Tell them to stay where I can't see them," she told Max.

"Hey, Meg, what's the matter with you? I've never seen you like this. Relax, will you? It's just a horse show."

"I am relaxed!" Megan snapped.

Amanda was starting her round. Jump for Joy began to canter toward the first fence. Megan watched intently. Suddenly, Megan realized that the fence Amanda was jumping was not the first fence on the course diagram stapled up near the in-gate. Amanda was jumping the wrong fence!

"Off course!" the ringmaster called out. "You are excused."

Amanda didn't seem to hear. She started to come around and jump the next line. "Amanda, come out!" Sharon called. "You're off course!" For a moment, it looked as though she intended to keep jumping, but then she hesitated and finally walked toward the gate.

Mrs. Sloane was waiting for Amanda. "Amanda-susloane, how could you? How could you mess up like that when you only need one more blue ribbon? After all the money Daddy and I spent getting you and this pony to win—all you have to do is stay on and remember the course!" Mrs. Sloane was nearly shrieking. Everyone around could hear her. For a second, Megan almost felt sorry for Amanda, but then she remembered Chloe.

Amanda's lower lip curled up and began to tremble. "Well, it's *hard*, Mama. It's a *hard* course to remember," she whined. "Sharon didn't tell me the course would be this hard. I can't remember such hard courses. I didn't know you had to go from that brown fence over there all the way around to this green one. How could anyone do that?"

"I see. Yes, I see now. That turn is simply too sharp. No one could possibly do that. Sharon— Sharon, may I have a word with you?"

Megan couldn't believe that Mrs. Sloane was actually going to complain about the course. Two other riders had gone since Amanda without any problem. Megan heard Sharon say to Mrs. Sloane, "The other children are getting around the course just fine."

Megan was on deck. She watched the child in

117

front of her finish her round and leave the ring. The paddock master called her number.

"Megan—" Max put a hand on his sister's leg to get her attention. "Don't worry. This is a piece of cake. Quit thinking about winning, and just *ride*." He gave her a friendly shove.

Megan gave Pixie a pat and trotted in. She took a deep breath and picked up a canter. *Relax, relax, relax*, she told herself with every stride. Suddenly, things began to click. She rode around the course just as she had done in that lesson, right down to the last fence. Pixie never even tossed her head! Megan finished up with a courtesy circle at the trot, walked, and let Pixie have a long rein. She gave her a big pat as she left the ring, but outside she bent forward and hugged her pony's neck hard. Pixie looked as proud of herself as her owner was. She arched her pretty neck and snorted with pleasure. When the ribbons were announced, Megan ended up taking fifth in the class.

"You should've won, Megan," Chloe told her. "You were the best."

Megan shook her head. "The competition is pretty tough in this division. I never show Pixie in the hunters, because she can be so quick and doesn't always carry her head down low like a Hunter pony should. I was really happy with how we did."

"But you really deserved to win," Chloe protested.

"I'd rather get fifth out of a big class like this

than first place in an easy class any old day," Megan explained.

The second jump class was starting. Megan asked Sharon to put her number in last. She wanted to give herself plenty of time to study the course and relax. She watched three ponies jump around, then Chloe, who was finally able to get Bo Peep to canter the whole course. She came out of the ring looking very happy with herself.

Soon the paddock master called Amanda's number "on deck," and Megan's "in the hole." That meant Megan was up after Amanda. She almost didn't want to watch Amanda jump, but then she did.

Amanda's mother had spent the last half hour drilling the jump course into her head. This time, Amanda got around the course. She came out of the ring looking relieved. Megan noticed that she didn't even reward her pony with a pat.

Then it was Megan's turn. She would have to put in another round just like her last one if she were going to beat Amanda. Could she do it? *Relax, relax, relax,* she was saying in her head with every stride. It seemed to work until the very last fence. Megan relaxed just an ounce too much, and Pixie took a long spot, leaving from farther away from the fence than she should. Megan was forced to grab mane to keep from getting left behind.

She was disappointed, mostly in herself for letting that mistake happen. Then they announced the ribbons. A handsome little chestnut with a white face won the class. Jump for Joy came in second, followed by Bo Peep! Chloe was ecstatic. Megan yelled and clapped. She was really happy for Chloe, but she was just as glad that Amanda still hadn't gotten her other blue ribbon. Now she had only one more chance at it. Amanda had to win the Under Saddle class, or she would be out of the Pony Hunter Championship.

The riders entered the ring. Megan immediately went to the far end to get in a space all by herself. That end of the ring was still very muddy from the rain the night before. She made a mental note to be very careful when she rode through it at the trot, and to stay out entirely when she was cantering. It felt very slippery even just walking.

The class began. Megan let Pixie pull the reins through her fingers and stretch her neck out. The little mare seemed to be getting more relaxed as the day wore on. If Megan rode carefully, she knew she could beat Amanda.

As she trotted toward the muddy end of the ring, she saw her parents standing with Max. Her mother was smiling. Her father waved. Max gave her a thumbs-up, and she grinned and let one thumb come up from the reins. Then she let Pixie pick her way through the sticky mud and trotted down the other side.

At the canter, Pixie stayed relaxed. Megan was so pleased, she didn't notice that she had ended up behind Amanda. They were heading for the muddy end of the arena. Megan realized she didn't want to be behind Amanda up there. She was about to move away when the pony in front of Amanda kicked out!

Jump for Joy shied to the left, almost cutting off Pixie. For a split second, Megan considered pulling up. But if she broke the canter, she would be eliminated, and then Amanda might win. Megan had to keep turning left to avoid crashing into Amanda, but somehow she managed to get out of the mud and keep cantering.

Out of the corner of her eye, Megan saw Amanda yank on her inside rein, trying to steer around Pixie's rump. Jump for Joy slipped in the mud, tried to recover, but lost his balance and skidded down on his hindquarter. For an awful moment, he floundered in the mud, then somehow, struggling mightily, he managed to get up. Megan heard the onlookers gasp. Jump for Joy was still trying his best to keep cantering, but something was wrong with his left front leg. Every time it touched the ground, he jerked it up in pain. After a moment, he just stopped and stood still, looking bewildered.

The judge must not have realized that the pony was injured, because the ringmaster didn't say to walk. Everyone had to keep cantering. Megan saw Mrs. Sloane leaning over the rail. "Amanda! Canter!" she was yelling. "You canter that pony NOW!"

Amanda heard her mother. For a second, the blank look lifted and was replaced by a look of fear. She lifted her bat and smacked the injured pony hard behind her leg. The sound seemed to carry over every other noise. Jump for Joy struggled once more to canter, groaning in pain as his useless leg refused to support his weight.

"Amanda! Hit him again!" Mrs. Sloane hissed. Amanda raised her bat again.

"STOP!" someone was yelling. "All walk," came the ringmaster's command. Megan walked and lined up with the other children in the middle of the ring. But no one was thinking about the class anymore. Everyone was watching Jump for Joy.

Sharon was already beside the pony. "Stop it!" she said. She snatched the bat from Amanda's upraised hand and threw it down. "Get off! Now! What's the matter with you? Can't you see this pony's hurt? Get off!"

Amanda seemed frozen. Sharon pushed her leg back to get her foot free of the stirrup. She grabbed Amanda by the jacket and pulled her out of the saddle, landing her unceremoniously in the mud. Amanda just sat there.

Sharon knelt and began feeling the pony's leg. When she touched the tendon in back of his leg, Jump for Joy flinched with pain. Sharon was shaking her head soberly. She waved at Jake over in the announcer's booth. "Jake! Call the vet!"

Mrs. Sloane came over and helped Amanda get up. For once, it seemed she had nothing to say. Sharon ran up Jump for Joy's stirrups and loosened his girth. She gently took the reins over his head and began to lead him out of the ring. Megan and the other children in the class sat on their ponies and watched as Jump for Joy picked his way bravely through the mud, limping horribly. It seemed to take forever for them to get across the arena and down to the gate. Megan realized she'd been holding her breath. She breathed out and in again sharply as the pony finally limped out.

When the results of the class were announced, Pixie had won, but Megan didn't feel very happy. There was a big lump in the back of her throat that felt somehow connected to her heart. And it just wouldn't go away. She had wanted to beat Amanda, to get even with her for hurting Chloe, but she'd never meant her or her pony any harm. Megan had the sickening feeling that the whole accident never would have happened if she had just pulled up and let Jump for Joy go in front of Pixie. She was sure the accident was all her fault!

12

MEGAN AND CHLOE WENT TO PUT PIXIE AND BO PEEP AWAY. Max and Keith helped them. Nobody seemed to be able to speak. Just as they were finishing up, Sharon came up the hill, leading Jump for Joy, who hobbled along behind her on three legs. Allie came over right away.

"It doesn't look good, Allie," Sharon said soberly. "Here, hold him, will you? I'm going out front to wait for Dr. Jordan."

Allie offered the pony water, which he slurped gratefully. Megan, Max, Keith, and Chloe gathered around, patting his neck and talking to him.

"Allie, what do you think it is?" Keith asked. "Is his leg broken?"

Allie shook her head. "Heck if I know. I sure hope not. I'd hate to see a fine little animal like this have to be put down. But the way he fell . . ." Allie shook her head again.

"Did you see it, Allie?" Megan asked in a low voice.

"I sure did. Looked like he hurt it trying to get back up and keep cantering. He's got a lot of heart, this little fella."

"Allie, I was right beside him when it happened. I went to pass, and the horse in front of him kicked at him because he was so close. Jump for Joy almost cut me off, but I guess he couldn't help it. I tried to get out of his way as best I could. . . ." Megan felt her voice begin to waver. "Was it my fault?"

"I saw what happened," Allie said. "I don't see how else you could've ridden it. I sure can't see how it could've been your fault."

"It wasn't your fault, Meg," Max consoled her. "I saw it, too. I don't know how you managed to keep cantering."

"Maybe I shouldn't have," Megan said. "If I had pulled up instead of cantering on, maybe Amanda would have had enough room to go around the pony that kicked."

"Amanda wasn't paying attention," Max said. "I was right there. She was riding like a robot. She never thought about moving away from that pony before it kicked out. Jump for Joy just tried to get away."

Megan sniffed and wiped at her eyes. She was glad nobody thought it was her fault, but she hoped Jump for Joy was going to be all right. She looked at her blue ribbon for a moment, then stuffed it into the pocket of her riding jacket. She didn't want to think about the class anymore.

In a few minutes, Sharon came down the aisle with Pepper Jordan, the veterinarian. "Dr. Pepper," as he was known throughout the county, was a tall, soft-spoken man with giant arm muscles from working around horses and cows so much. He wore baggy coveralls splattered with mud and blood. His face was kind, with tons of creases, most of them around his eyes and mouth from laughing a lot. When he saw the pony, though, the furrows in his forehead deepened in a frown of concern.

"What happened?" he asked, setting down his bag.

He listened intently as Sharon explained how the pony had been injured. Then he squatted down and went to work examining the leg. The children peered over his shoulder, trying to watch without getting shooed out of the way. He felt up and down the leg, watching for the pony's reaction. He hooked up the ultrasound equipment, and a picture of the muscles and bones inside the pony's leg appeared on the monitor. When he had finished, he gave Jump for Joy a sympathetic pat and stood up. "Who owns the pony?" he asked.

"I do," Mrs. Sloane said. She came from the second aisle with her daughter. Both of them were drinking diet sodas. "Well, what do we have to do to fix him?" she joked.

Dr. Pepper smiled politely. Then he grew serious. "This pony has torn his suspensory ligament. It's as bad a tear as I've ever seen," he said. He waited for Mrs. Sloane to respond.

Mrs. Sloane took a sip of her soda. "Ger-ald!" she called. "Gerald, do come out here."

A large, balding man in a suit came out of the barn office. His face was very red and sweaty, and he looked completely irritated, as if finding himself in a barn was the most annoying thing that had happened to him all day. Max was sure the man must be Amanda's father. He had the same pouty expression as his daughter, and the same mean little eyes.

Mrs. Sloane kept her eyes on Dr. Pepper. "Gerald, dear, perhaps you ought to hear this. This *doctor*—she emphasized the word as if she didn't believe it but was trying to be polite—"says that our Mandy's pony is severely injured."

"Well, what's the matter with 'im?" Gerald Sloane barked. He pulled out a handkerchief and dabbed angrily at his sweaty face. "Mandy, honey, go get Daddy a diet drink, won't you, precious?" Mr. Sloane handed Amanda some change and gave her a little shove in the direction of the soda machine.

"This pony's torn his suspensory ligament," Dr. Pepper told Amanda's father. "And it's a bad one. He'll need complete stall rest at first, then lots of careful hand-walking, then some pasture rest. I can't be sure, but he might never jump again."

"Mandy!" Gerald Sloane yelled. "You hurry up with that soda."

Amanda scurried back with a diet soda and

handed it to her father. He opened it and began to gulp. He downed half the soda and burped loudly. Then, turning to the doctor, he said, "Well, now, just how much time are we talkin' here, before this critter can git back to work? A week? Two?"

Dr. Pepper scratched his head and smoothed his hair back. Then he spoke. "I'm afraid we're talking a lot more than just a week or two here. An injury like this heals very slowly. I don't believe you can figure on having him back for three to six months."

Gerald Sloane scowled. He wiped his sweaty forehead again. "Well now, I can't be payin' board and feed on a critter that my Mandy can't even ride, can I? And I don't reckon nobody will buy him with that leg busted up like that, am I right?" He gulped down the rest of the soda and handed the can to his wife. "Put him down," he said.

All that time, Megan had been watching Amanda. She had sipped at her soda and shifted her weight impatiently from one foot to another. She hadn't even been interested in seeing the ultrasound. But at her father's words, she suddenly reacted.

"No!" Amanda shrieked. "Daddy, no! You can't put him down! He's the best pony I ever had! What will I do?" she pleaded.

"Now, now, sugar. You don't want this ol' broken-down pony. Daddy will buy you a new one!" He patted his daughter on the head and turned to his wife. "Let's go, Pamela. It's hot in this dadgum barn."

Megan, Max, Chloe, and Keith all exchanged

horrified looks. They couldn't believe that Mr. Sloane was willing simply to put Jump for Joy down after he'd been such a good pony. Now Megan really did feel sorry for Amanda. Maybe she couldn't help being the way she was, with such awful parents.

"Mr. Sloane, are you sure?" Sharon said. "There's a chance this'll heal completely, with the right treatment. It seems a shame just to put this pony down after he's been so good for Amanda."

Mr. Sloane didn't even turn around. He was walking lazily down the aisle toward the parking area. "All I do is pay board and vet bills and shoe-ing bills on these dad-gummed horses. I'll be blamed if I'll pay for one that ain't workin' for me. If I had my gun, I'd put him out of his misery right now—then I wouldn't have to pay the vet to do it. Put him down right now, and let me know when it's done. I'll be waitin' in my car."

Mrs. Sloane headed up the aisle after her husband. Amanda stood uncertainly, glancing from the pony to the shocked faces of the other children. Dr. Pepper stood with his hands on his hips, watching the Sloanes walk away. Allie stared at the floor.

"Amanda, don't you think if you spoke to your parents, they might reconsider?" Sharon asked her. "You love this pony, don't you?"

They all looked to see what Amanda would do. Megan knew what she would do—she'd threaten to throw herself down in the middle of the highway before she'd let her parents have her pony put down.

Amanda opened her mouth to speak, then closed it again. She stared at the pony's swollen leg.

"Amanda, you come this instant, you hear?" Mrs. Sloane called from the end of the aisle. "You know how Daddy hates to wait."

"Amanda?" Sharon prompted.

"My daddy will buy me a new one," she said at last, and followed her mother outside.

They were all silent. Sharon sighed. "Well, let's get this thing over with," she said.

"Where do you want to do it?" Dr. Pepper asked Sharon.

"Let's take him around the side of the barn, over by the honeysuckle. That way, nobody from the show can see him. The fewer people know about this, the better."

Megan had forgotten that the horse show was still going on. Just then, a pretty woman in a flowered dress came into the barn. She was carrying a little blond boy with a very dirty face.

"Chloe, there you are. We've been looking all over for you. I wanted to tell you how proud I am of your riding. You looked so good out there!" She beamed at Chloe.

"Oh, Mama . . ." Chloe threw her arms around her mother and sobbed. Chloe's little brother patted her head worriedly.

"Chloe, he won't suffer. It'll be over in a second,"

Dr. Pepper told her. He explained to Chloe's mother what was about to happen.

Megan couldn't imagine being a veterinarian and having to do the job Dr. Pepper was about to do. She had always thought of vets as people who tried to save animals. Dr. Pepper squeezed Chloe's shoulder, then picked up his bag and headed out the way Allie had gone. Megan, Max, and Keith started to follow them out. Sharon turned around.

"Oh, no. You three stay right here," she told them.

They stood in the aisle. "Come on," Keith said. "Let's go around the other way. I can't just sit here and wait."

They followed him around to the back of the barn, moving quietly along the fence line. They crouched behind the honeysuckle vine and watched as Dr. Pepper took a syringe out of his bag and prepared the injection that would end the pony's life.

Jump for Joy stood with his head drooping. His hurt leg trembled slightly as he held it up. Sharon took hold of his halter, shaking her head in disgust. Allie stared off to the side. It was the first time Megan had seen her look uncomfortable. Dr. Pepper held up the syringe.

Megan felt the lump in her throat get so big she could hardly breathe. She couldn't believe what she was about to see. She felt tears running down her cheeks. She wasn't sure she wanted to watch anymore, but she couldn't tear her eyes off the horrifying scene before her. For the first time since she was very small, she reached out and took her brother's hand. She felt Max squeeze her own hand very tightly.

Dr. Pepper pinched a fold of Jump for Joy's skin between his fingers and felt for a vein. He lifted the syringe and held it poised over the pony's neck.

"WAIT!" Megan screamed. She burst out of the bushes.

"What's she doing?" Max and Keith exchanged puzzled looks. Megan ran to Sharon and began talking rapidly. Sharon frowned at first, then listened intently to what Megan was saying and nodded. Dr. Pepper smiled and let go of Jump for Joy's neck.

The Sloanes' big, shiny car sat at the top of the driveway with the engine running. Sharon rapped on the window, and Mr. Sloane rolled it down just enough for her to speak through. In another second, Mr. Sloane passed a paper through the crack to Sharon, rolled up the window, and drove off. Sharon came back with Megan, holding the paper and grinning. Max and Keith were waiting with curious expressions.

"What happened?" Max asked. "Did Mr. Sloane change his mind?"

"You might say that," Sharon answered. She never showed much emotion, but Max thought she looked as pleased as anyone could.

Just then, Chloe came out of the barn with her mother and her little brother. She stopped when she saw all of them standing there. "Is . . . is it done?" she asked, her voice breaking.

Sharon handed Chloe the paper Gerald Sloane had given her. "Here you go, Chloe. This is for you."

Chloe unfolded it, perplexed, and began to read. "It's his registration papers," she said. "Huh?" Her green eyes opened very wide. "It says 'owner— Chloe Goodman'! How can that be?" She looked up from Sharon to Dr. Pepper. "What does this mean?"

"It was Megan's quick thinking," Sharon explained. "She figured the Sloanes just wanted to get rid of the pony so they wouldn't have to fool with his long recovery. Gerald signed the papers over to you. He was just glad not to have to pay to have him put down. Chloe, Jump for Joy is yours if you want him."

Dr. Pepper led the pony slowly out from behind the barn. Chloe looked from the pony to Sharon to Megan, as if she couldn't quite believe what they were telling her.

"If I want him? Of course I want him! Mom, can I?" Chloe turned to her mother with a pleading look.

"Chloe, honey, you know we can't afford to pay for the board." Chloe's face fell. She started to hand the paper back to Sharon.

"We'll work something out," Sharon offered.

"Now that you can pull manes and braid, maybe you can work off his board. And there are always stalls to muck and tack to clean."

"Really? You'd really let me work it off? Mom? Can I?"

Chloe's mother nodded her approval.

"Oh, my goodness, I can't believe this is really happening! Thank you so much!" Chloe hugged Sharon hard. "This is the best day of my whole entire life!" She hugged Megan. She was heading for Max and Keith, but they backed away, shaking their heads.

"Oh, no, not us!" they warned her.

"I'll take the best care of you, I promise," Chloe whispered to Jump for Joy. She kissed the pony gently on his soft, white nose, and he rested his head on her shoulder with a sigh.

They all went into the barn. At the door, Megan paused. "Oh, look, Max!" Megan pointed to the paddock nearest the barn, where four little foals romped and played. They were the same four babies Megan and Max had seen on their first day at Thistle Ridge.

Megan and Max stood in the doorway together and watched the foals. "You know," Max said, "this turned out to be an okay place after all."

Just then, the little bay filly with the white star stopped playing. She walked daintily to the paddock fence and stood facing the door where Megan and Max were standing. She seemed to be looking right at Megan. "Look, Max," Megan said softly. "She wants to be friends."

"We all want to be friends," Max said. "Come on, Megan, let's go find Chloe and Keith." They turned and went into the main barn of Thistle Ridge Farm, where more adventures were waiting for them.

About the Author

ALLISON ESTES grew up in Oxford, Mississippi. She wrote, bound, and illustrated her first book when she was five years old, learned to drive her grandfather's truck when she was eight, and got her first pony when she was ten. She has been writing, driving trucks, and riding horses ever since.

Allison is a trainer at Claremont Riding Academy, the only riding stable in New York City. She currently lives in Manhattan with her seven-year-old daughter, Megan, who spends every spare moment around, under, or on horses.

SADDLE UP FOR MORE ADVENTURES WITH MEGAN, MAX, CHLOE, KEITH, AND AMANDA IN

GHOST OF THISTLE RIDGE

When an overnight camp-out near an old barn ends in Amanda's disappearance, Megan starts to believe the stories about the ghost of a young girl that wanders the pastures of Thistle Ridge Farm. Determined to help find the missing Amanda and Prince Charming, her horse, Megan, Max, Chloe, and Keith set out to search for clues. Separated from the others, Megan discovers an old diary that reveals the secrets of the haunted barn and spooky grave-yard nearby. But can this voice from the past lead Megan to Amanda before time runs out?